PAST UNBECOMING

PAST
UNBECOMING

NICK EVERARD

The Book Guild Ltd

First published in Great Britain in 2023 by
The Book Guild Ltd
Unit E2 Airfield Business Park,
Harrison Road, Market Harborough,
Leicestershire. LE16 7UL
Tel: 0116 2792299
www.bookguild.co.uk
Email: info@bookguild.co.uk
Twitter: @bookguild

Typeset in 11pt Minion Pro

Printed on FSC accredited paper
Printed and bound in Great Britain by 4edge Limited

ISBN 978 1915603 739

British Library Cataloguing in Publication Data.
A catalogue record for this book is available from the British Library.

Dedicated to my fine contemporaries in the 9th/12th Royal Lancers (1977 – 1999), and to their present day successors in The Royal Lancers: any scandals in the distinguished Second World War service of their forbears are long buried, and no resemblance is intended to anyone, living or dead.

I thank my good friends Charlie and Chris for their thoughtful comments on the draft manuscript, which greatly improved it.

Above all I am grateful once more to my dear Kiki; a loyal Army wife for sixteen years.

Milo RIP 2022

Nick Everard is a former Army officer who has worked subsequently in the City, schools adventure travel and recruiting / headhunting. He became Regimental Secretary of The Royal Lancers in July 2021. Nick is married to Kiki, and lives on the Leicestershire / Northamptonshire border close to Market Harborough. They have two grown children. 'Past Unbecoming' is his second novel: the first ('Clean Kill') was published by The Book Guild in May 2022.

CHAPTER ONE

I f you're lucky enough to be able to retire at forty-eight, as I was, then you need something to do. So once I recognised that, I did what I'd always done when thinking about the next steps in my City career – I was open about it, and asked trusted friends for advice or ideas.

Quite a lot of those friends were people I'd met during my eight-year Short Service Commission in the Army, many years before. If you are aiming to become a combat soldier you don't really join the Army of course: you join a Regiment, and Regiments are proudly distinct tribes.

My fellow officers in Prince Rupert's Horse were (and are) a pretty eclectic bunch: a few stayed the course, and some of them went on to high military rank; others (like me) went into the City after a few years, and flourished – or otherwise.

Beyond that there are a couple of titled landowners, a former cabinet minister, a few captains of industry, a rather successful actor, a photographer, an Anglican clergyman, a (hopefully) recovering alcoholic, and a former jailbird amongst my generation. Provided they were broadly competent, the Regiment of my time valued individuality (indeed sometimes outright eccentricity) amongst its officers, taking its inspiration from the great Royalist cavalryman it was named for – although we were now mounted on tanks rather than horses, and had been since the 1930s.

With very few exceptions, people of similar vintage tended in my day to stay in touch once they left, and probably still do. It was a fine thing to be in your early twenties, loaded with unaccustomed responsibility, and sometimes (not often enough, for most of us) going to 'interesting' places: we all valued the comradeship of those we shared such youthful adventures with; we could feel ourselves growing up and even today we snap straight back to being twenty-something again when two or more of us are gathered together.

Friends for life: it's a cliché of course, but clichés are rooted in truth. And you tend to know the strengths and weaknesses of such people pretty well; even those you haven't seen for a bit.

So against that background I had lunch with Charlie Manning in a country pub, not far from the Regiment's Home Headquarters in Newark, one fine day in May 2005.

Charlie was nearly five years older than me, which is just about close enough to call a contemporary, though he'd been pretty difficult for my first year or so. It's changed now, with almost all officers being graduates, but that wasn't the case in the Army of the early eighties, at least in Rupert's. Most people (Charlie included) hadn't been to university, so were slightly resentful of those who had: we arrived 'late', laden with additional seniority.

It was very much the 'new boy at boarding school'

syndrome: you had to earn acceptance. Nothing Flashman-esque; people just kept their distance for a while. However, I was a boarding school veteran, so it was nothing new to me, and I knew it would pass.

Thus Charlie and I were firm friends now, and had been for nearly twenty-five years.

***

Charlie was then the Regimental Secretary, running Home Headquarters, and if you are to understand my tale then that role needs brief explanation.

It's a Civil Service post, though since the job requires knowledge of the Regiment and its ethos it's usually filled by a retired former officer, who may have served anything from three years to thirty.

The Regimental Secretary supports the Colonel of the Regiment: a part-time, unpaid appointment invariably filled by a distinguished former regimental officer, often retired but sometimes still serving in the Army in high rank.

The Colonel sets standards, and broad ongoing regimental policy: not the same thing as the Commanding Officer, a Lieutenant Colonel who runs the serving Regiment day to day, though almost certainly the Colonel of the Regiment would once have been Commanding Officer himself.

I suppose in civilian terms one is the Non-Executive Chairman of a firm of 600 people, and the other the Chief Executive.

If all that's not clear then by all means read it again, and welcome to the regimental system.

A degree of liaison with the office of the Colonel in Chief

(invariably a Royal) is also involved in the Secretary's role: ours has been the King since his investiture as Prince of Wales in 1969.

Beyond this: welfare; commemorative events; dinners; archives; the museum; finance; chattels; managing potential officers; secretary to the trustees – that sort of thing. It's a continuity function, which the serving Regiment, wherever it happens to be (which was Germany in 2005; it plays no part in this story) simply isn't set up to handle.

And that's all you need to know.

Charlie had done all this for about four years by the time of our meeting. He'd left the Army as a well-liked but not particularly successful Major in his mid-forties, and for a few years thereafter became a gentleman farmer on the estate which his wealthy wife, Sian, had inherited. That was until both she and the farm manager, acting in concert, had tactfully eased him out.

Some said that there was rather more to their alliance than this, since the marriage ended at the same time, but Charlie's pals paid no heed to such scurrilous rumours and were delighted when he took up the Regimental Secretary position upon the retirement of his predecessor, Ron Stiller.

Our lunch was one of several I had set up with assorted friends for the reasons spelt out above, and in truth I didn't expect a great deal to come of it: I hadn't seen Charlie for a couple of years and thought it would be fun just to catch up. So we did that for much of the meal, gossiping about all and sundry: we were onto the coffee before he gave me the moment I needed after a brief lull in the conversation.

'Didn't you say when you called that there was something you wanted to ask me?' he asked quietly.

I noticed as he did so that he had the beginnings of a double chin, and had lost quite a lot of his once abundant brown hair. Middle age creeps up on all of us.

'Yes,' I replied. 'There is.'

Charlie stayed silent whilst I marshalled my thoughts.

'The fact is – I'm now retired from full-time work,' I began.

'Lucky you,' replied Charlie. He knew that my three fellow directors and I had recently sold the boutique fund management firm we had set up in 1992 for a large amount.

'Yes – but I need things to do. Not necessarily full-time things, nor things that pay hugely. Interesting things. Necessary things. Things that will keep me out from under Kate's feet,' I said

'Charitable work, perhaps? Or running a charity?' mused Charlie.

I waved this away. 'I've probably got something going in that line already. What I'd like to do is build a portfolio career of worthwhile roles that interest me. Isn't there anything I could help the Regiment with? Not permanent: just a temporary task perhaps?'

Charlie began to shake his head resignedly, and then stopped. For the very first time in my life I saw someone actually struck by a lightbulb moment.

'There just might be something,' he said, after a few seconds of consideration.

'What?'

There was a brief shake of the head. 'Let me run it past Jazzer first.'

***

5

Lieutenant General Sir Jasper Montagnon KCB, DSO, MBE was the then Colonel of the Regiment – an appointment people usually held for about five years. He rang me at home a few days later.

'Dom – it's Jazzer,' he said, with his usual abrupt forcefulness.

'Good evening, Colonel,' I replied.

'Oh, don't worry about all that,' he said impatiently, knowing that even long-departed officers like me often used the title for whoever held the appointment, even if they were friends (or at least acquaintances) of many years' standing.

'Well – good evening, then,' I said, and waited.

'Evening. Now look – Charlie tells me that you're happy to help with our project.'

'Not quite. I said that in principle I'd be happy to help with something. He didn't tell me what it was. Said he had to discuss it with you first.'

Jazzer paused for a moment.

'Well, he's done that.' That being the case, my acceptance seemed to him a mere formality.

'What is it?' I persisted.

'Oh – a bit of writing. You were always good at that, I recall.'

'Can you tell me a little more?'

I sensed a moment of bafflement at such insubordination the other end. Then, having weighed up the factors in traditional military fashion, a course of action was decided upon.

'Much better face to face. And probably easier here. Could you manage lunch this Saturday?'

There was no mention of bringing Kate; not that she'd

have welcomed a trip from Leicestershire to Wiltshire simply for a meal, so that was probably a blessing.

'Fine – I look forward to it. Twelve-thirty?'

'Twelve-thirty for one. You know where we are. Casual. Talk then.'

Typically, the phone went down before I had a chance to reply. I smiled indulgently and was pouring myself a whisky when Kate appeared in the drawing room.

'Who was that?'

'Jazzer. Lunch on Saturday. Wants me to do something.'

I detected the beginnings of a forceful reaction and stayed her with my hand.

'Don't worry: you're in the clear.'

I knew the 'just as well' look that followed: Kate tolerated my military friends, but we'd married after I had left the Army, so she didn't know them well, and didn't really care to. They came from a pre-Kate era. She picked up the magazine she had come in for and turned on her heel.

'Supper in fifteen minutes,' she said over her shoulder.

'Fine,' I said to the receding jeans-clad figure, or at least to its shapely posterior.

I settled into my armchair, took a sip and began to reflect upon the dynamic character I'd just been talking to.

Jazzer had joined the Army as a career, unlike most of us, and it was soon apparent that he was destined for great things. Powerfully built, charismatic and with a good measure of natural charm when he chose to use it, he was a natural leader who took his profession seriously.

About the same age as Charlie, though a lot more successful, he'd done all the 'right' career jobs: ADC to a Major General; a rather daunting Adjutant of the Regiment when I first arrived; something suitably high-powered in HQ British Army of the Rhine after Staff College. He'd also picked up an MBE for his performance as a Squadron Leader (Cavalry Regiments have Squadrons; the equivalent of Infantry Companies) over a six-month tour in Northern Ireland, and a DSO during the Kosovo campaign, during which he had led the Regiment with distinction as its Commanding Officer. He'd since commanded both a Brigade and a Division.

He was the recently appointed Director of something or other in the Ministry of Defence when he rang – it was probably his last appointment before retiring from the Army.

Unlike most Generals, Jazzer was pretty much what central casting would come up with if asked to produce one. It would be interesting to know what he wanted me to do – and also, I recognised even then, hard to turn such a powerful personality down.

***

The Montagnons owned a country house outside the village of Pewsey, bought five years or so before.

Since an increasing amount of the Army's post-Cold War infrastructure was based around Salisbury Plain, they had chosen to settle there once Jazzer reached a certain level of seniority in the hope of achieving domestic stability: better that than the constant upheavals between married quarters of variable quality which were often necessary at more junior levels.

It had worked, more or less, though Charlie had told me that Jazzer was commuting weekly to London in his current Ministry of Defence role.

I'd only been to the Pewsey house once before, and that at night, so I took the place in properly for the first time as I drove through the gates that sunny Saturday. It was Georgian, with classic symmetry and typical sash windows, and sat at the end of a drive of thirty yards or so: not excessive in size, but certainly comfortable, and benefiting from a new coat of white paint if I was not mistaken. The lawns looked immaculate – senior officers still got plenty of domestic assistance in those days, though no doubt 'austerity' has done for all that now.

I parked on the gravel, and saw the man himself grinning at me as I emerged from my Alfa, standing between the two pillars of the portico. With his powerful build and curly fair hair he looked like some Hollywood version of Samson about to tear down the temple.

'Dom,' he said, advancing down the steps in shirtsleeves, hand outstretched. 'My dear chap. So good of you to come.'

I shrugged. 'When the Colonel summons...'

Jazzer laughed, genuinely – always one of his more attractive traits; he clearly didn't expect me to continue using that title. Then I saw him look me up and down. I was rather more formally dressed than him, wearing a jacket, and he noticed straightaway.

'You're rather smart. Casual, I said.'

Back in the eighties, when I'd been serving, 'casual' might mean a blazer rather than a suit. I wasn't quite sure how much Jazzer had moved with the times, so being on his home turf had erred on the side of caution.

'Well, you're a Knight of the Realm these days. One has to show respect,' I said, with a hint of a smile.

'Oh, bollocks to all that, you bloody City slicker. Come on in.'

He led the way up the steps and I found myself in the hallway, which contained Mary.

Whereas Jazzer took his knighthood lightly, I'd heard that Mary was pretty serious about being Lady Mary. She was roughly my age, and five or six years younger than her husband: well preserved, and still very much recognisable as the slim, brunette newlywed whom we'd all welcomed into the regimental family during my final year. However, now there was an unmistakeable hauteur about her. I thought initially it might be the unfamiliar short hairstyle, but it was more than that.

'Hello, Dom,' she said quietly, and offered herself for a chaste kiss.

I grabbed her in a bear hug with a lecherous roar instead, which she'd have loved fifteen years earlier, but now I felt her stiffen and pull deftly away with a pained smile. Mistake.

Jazzer noticed her reaction, and I could see that he was a little embarrassed: there was a rather strained silence for a moment until his House Sergeant appeared with a bottle of champagne on a tray, with three flutes already poured. Jazzer took two of them, handed one to Mary and another to me, grabbed the bottle and the other glass from the tray, and led us through to the drawing room without a backward glance. I ushered Mary tactfully through the doorway ahead of me, and received a graceful but serious nod in return.

The drawing room was very formally furnished, but without any military mementoes at all, which surprised me. On the far wall some French windows led us through to a terrace, which overlooked a delightful lawned garden, and there we all settled down.

It was pretty conventional 'catch up' chit chat, though

pleasant enough for all that. Mary was polite, but remained fairly aloof: how was dear Kate; hadn't she heard we might be moving; what was I planning to do now etc. Jazzer butted in from time with anecdotes about someone or other; usually fairly close to the knuckle. Nothing very memorable, until Mary looked at him sharply after the third of these.

'You can save all that for lunch,' she said pointedly to her husband.

He looked away, and took a sip of his drink. I knew him well enough to know that he was irritated.

'Why, aren't you joining us?' I said as light-heartedly as I could, in an attempt to defuse things.

Mary stood, and drained her champagne.

'I wouldn't dream of it,' she said decisively, and replaced the glass carefully on the table.

'See you later, perhaps, Dom.' The smile seemed genuine enough, because Mary was an excellent hostess, but it was directed solely at me.

She turned and vanished through the French windows, leaving Jazzer and I looking awkwardly at each other.

CHAPTER TWO

Lunch was in the dining room, which seemed like slight overkill, and we sat at ninety degrees to each other at the end of the long table. A simple cottage pie was laid out on a sideboard, together with vegetables, and Jazzer and I helped ourselves. He offered a rather decent looking claret to accompany it, which I regretfully declined after my champagne since I had to drive. I settled for water.

Jazzer faced no such constraint, and poured himself a large glass.

I'd carefully avoided any reaction to the earlier apparent spat with Mary, beyond thinking that it had probably originated in some silly domestic squabble before I arrived, and we continued talking generalities whilst we settled at the table.

There was a bit of gossip about the Regiment, shortly to deploy from Germany to Bosnia on an operational tour: it was now commanded by someone I remembered arriving in my final year looking about sixteen, but Bosnia was pretty old hat by 2005, and that particular line of conversation soon fizzled out.

Never one to beat about the bush, Jazzer then cut straight to the point.

'I suppose I'd better tell you what all this is about,' he said, before taking his first mouthful.

I followed suit. The pie was delicious.

'Well, yes: that's rather the point of me being here,' I replied.

He took another mouthful, and then a sip of wine.

'How's your regimental history?'

He looked at me forcefully, awaiting an answer. I paused to reflect, rather surprised.

'Fair enough, I suppose. A bit rusty. It wouldn't withstand detailed questioning.'

He shook his head. 'Not a problem. World War Two?'

I took a sip of water.

'I know the outline. France in 1940; then the desert; then back to England at Monty's insistence to take part in D-Day. From there, on into Germany.'

Jazzer nodded as he ate. 'That's about the size of it. Some people weren't too happy after Africa. Thought it was time other buggers took their turn.'

I shrugged. 'Fair enough. Quite a bit of the Army had been sitting in England for years doing sod all. Monty wanted some of his experienced armoured Regiments for the invasion.'

'How well does the regimental history cover those years, do you think?'

I was on pretty shaky ground here. As a young, newly arrived Lieutenant I'd been directed to read regimental history, and then questioned on it by the Adjutant – one Captain Jasper Montagnon. But although I'd been happy enough to do so at the time (indeed had rather enjoyed it), that was over twenty-five years ago.

'Can't comment – too long since I've read it.'

'Can you remember who wrote it?'

I thought for a moment.

'Billy Mullins, wasn't it?'

Billy was a long-serving bachelor who had retired from the Army as a Major under faintly mysterious circumstances in the fifties, but I had known him well: being very sociable, he was still attending regimental dinners in the eighties, when I'd been around. There was always a faint hint of scandal around him – if not drink, then horses, and perhaps more, so rumour had it. But it was tolerated, because Billy was Billy: he was invariably amusing; he'd had a good war, including a Military Cross, and his knowledge of the Regiment and its history was acknowledged to be second to none. He'd died about twelve years before: I'd gone to his funeral, and not just out of duty.

'Yes – Billy. However, Billy was wounded in Tunisia in 1943, right at the end of the Africa campaign – pretty badly, too. Even when he recovered he was kept on Home establishment as an instructor. So he never served with the Regiment during D-Day and beyond. He only came back to us post war.'

'So what?'

Jazzer looked thoughtful for a moment.

'The thing is – when the time came for someone to write the history of Prince Rupert's Horse from 1939 till 1945, he was the obvious choice. He was also the only volunteer. It was either that, or hire a professional writer, who wouldn't have

14

understood us, or had people's trust. The regimental elders of the day backed Billy. Of course, they all knew him well.'

'So what's the issue? He did a fine job, didn't he?'

'Up to a point. Billy had been in France in 1940, and he'd been in Africa. He knew how things were in those places; he knew the personalities, and he could bring it all to life with anecdotes, of which he was a master, as you know.'

'Yes – he was.'

Jazzer nodded. 'The trouble was, he couldn't do that with D-Day and beyond, because he hadn't been there. Nor do I think he had much interest. So if you read what he wrote about that final period of the war, it's very thin by comparison with the earlier stuff. To be frank, he went through the motions.'

'I never noticed.'

'That's because you were idle, and never read it properly.' It was said with a twinkle in his eye.

'Very probably,' I said, accepting the rebuke. 'And I'll take your word for all this. So where do I come in?'

'I want someone to re-write the regimental history over that period – from the return to England after Africa till the end of the war. Would you consider doing that, and doing it justice? I know you're a good writer.'

It was true that I'd had several well-received articles published in the financial press, and that I enjoyed writing, unlike many. It was something I was aiming to do more of now that I was a free agent, without at this early stage of my post-City career being any more specific than that.

So it might fit well, and beyond that I was also rather flattered. I thought for a moment.

'When would you need this completed?'

'Well, Billy's original history came out in 1958. So I rather hoped we might have it ready by the fiftieth anniversary: three years' time. Ample, I hope. And you wouldn't need to do it full time: run it in tandem with whatever else you're doing these days.'

I took my last mouthful, then some more water, and sat back reflectively.

'Will you do it?' I couldn't recall Jazzer pleading with me ever before, and savoured the unaccustomed feeling, letting him wait for a few seconds.

'Yes, in principle.'

'Excellent. You'll make a fine job of it, I know.'

The unsaid implication was 'you'd better make a fine job of it.' Jazzer got up, and helped himself to some more cottage pie. Still lean and fit, he could well afford a healthy appetite.

'I'm glad that's settled,' he said firmly, returning to the table. 'Oh sorry – do you want any more too?'

I shook my head. 'No thanks, Jazzer. Delicious. But look, where do I start? Where's all the original material?'

He sat down and took another mouthful.

'Well, you can start right here. There are boxes of stuff. Take it all away with you.'

People don't believe me now, but it was only then that I remembered who had commanded the Regiment from shortly after D-Day until the end of the war.

Lieutenant Colonel Giles Montagnon, DSO and bar, MC. Jazzer's father.

***

Jazzer obviously had faith in his persuasive powers, because when he led me through to his study after lunch I saw that the family regimental archive was all boxed up and ready for me. There were three cardboard boxes, all open at the top, and mostly containing rather moth-eaten orange loose-leaf folders which clearly dated from a couple of generations ago. I could also see a few notebooks, a lever-arch file, and some old maps.

I took it all in.

'Have you read all this?' I asked, genuinely curious. 'To be honest, I'd forgotten that your father was commanding for most of that period.'

Jazzer shrugged. 'Dabbled, I think you could say. No more than that.'

He saw my surprise, and spread his hands expansively. 'Look, I don't think it's any great secret that my father and I had a somewhat fraught relationship. He was pretty strong willed, and —'

'You are too,' I interjected.

He grinned ruefully. 'I suppose I am. Chip off the old block. We were probably too alike.'

I picked up something from one of the boxes at random. It appeared to be a bundle of letters, with the envelopes all addressed in the elegant formal handwriting which most of the wartime generation had espoused, now largely a thing of the past.

'You must be curious about it, surely? On purely military grounds?' I said, showing him.

Jazzer shrugged. 'Not really. A lot of it is probably personal, like those letters, and completely irrelevant.'

'Well, I'd like to be the judge of that, if I'm to tell the full story. Are you saying that I have carte blanche to use all of this?'

'I suppose that's what you want if you are to take it on?'

17

'Yes.'

'Well then, so be it. Obviously I'd like to see the draft before we go to print, but till then – use whatever you like.'

I put the bundle back in the box.

'When did your father die?' I asked. 'I can't recall going to the funeral. Must have been a big regimental do: last of the wartime Commanding Officers.'

'December 1990. He was seventy-eight. Actually it wasn't that big – firstly because that's what he wanted, and secondly because the Regiment was in Kuwait: it was just before Desert Storm. Which I missed,' he said regretfully.

'Though I was very involved in who the British Army sent there,' he added, after a pause. He sounded almost defensive.

'Well, I was out of the Army by then. Sorry I missed the funeral though. Maybe I was abroad: I often was in those days. What about your mother?'

I said this only since it seemed to be the logical continuation of the conversation; not out of any genuine curiosity. I could only remember meeting her once, during an 'Old Comrades' visit to the Regiment in Germany in the eighties. Nonetheless, I was surprised by the answer.

'Oh, she's still knocking about. Here, in fact.'

He saw my surprised reaction, and beckoned me over to the study window, which faced onto a small lawn off the side of the house: we hadn't been able to see it from the terrace before lunch.

'Look,' he indicated. 'It's one of the main reasons we bought this place.'

The window overlooked a neat little bungalow some thirty yards away across the lawn: no more than two bedrooms, I assessed.

18

'That's her lair. She's entirely self-sufficient, and still drives much too fast. Always has.'

'Well – good for her,' I responded. 'Both my folks are gone I'm afraid. Kate's mum is still around though.'

'I'll help you get all this into the car,' said Jazzer, changing tack abruptly. It seemed it was time for me to go.

Two loads each, and I was ready to leave, apart from one thing. Jazzer saw me casting around.

'I ought to say goodbye to Mary...' I began.

He waved this away. 'Don't worry. God knows where she is.'

'Maybe I should just pop inside...?'

'Look – I said it was OK,' he replied, in a tone which brooked no argument.

'All right. If you're sure. Thank you very much for an excellent lunch, anyway, and please pass that on to Mary,' I said, opening my car door.

Jazzer smiled, all bonhomie again. 'It was great to see you, Dom. And thank you for taking this on.'

He headed towards the steps, and waved from the top one as I reversed around, then he headed inside. I took a final look at the house as I put the car into gear.

It was only a glimpse, and at the time I thought I'd imagined it, because of the glass. I'm still not sure.

Mary seemed to be watching me from the first floor, a few feet back from the window. I thought I saw her wave her hand briefly in farewell, but the reflection made it hard to tell.

***

Whilst driving home I had slight reservations about what I'd taken on, not improved by Kate's reaction once she heard.

'I don't suppose there's any money in it,' she said. 'Sounds like a fearful bore.'

I bridled a bit at this. Kate has always been rather insecure about financial matters, having had a father who'd drunk away most of what wealth he had, leaving her mother an impecunious widow.

'We don't actually need any more money, unless you want me to buy a private jet,' I pointed out. 'We're sitting on fourteen million. And I'll find it interesting.'

I wasn't actually sure I would do, but didn't want to leave a loophole in my argument. Kate took the mild rebuke in her stride and nodded graciously.

'So how will you go about it?'

I finished pouring myself a beer after a long day, and thought about this fairly pertinent question whilst I did so. Kate already had a glass of something. We settled down together on opposite sides of the kitchen island.

'Not sure. I think the first thing is to digest what Jazzer's given me. I'll take it from there.'

'But that won't be the whole story, will it?'

'Undoubtedly not. But it's a start point. And it'll tell me quite a bit about his father, who's clearly central to the whole thing.'

Kate looked dubious.

'That's going to be rather delicate, isn't it?'

I waved this away as confidently as I could, though not without a vague feeling that she might be right.

'No. Don't think so. I'll obviously be aware of potential sensitivities, but it's common knowledge that he did an outstanding job. Monty awarded him his second DSO personally.'

'Did you ever meet him?'

'Yes, but only at regimental dinners and the like whilst I was still serving,' I replied. 'He must have been well into his seventies by then. We were all rather in awe of him.'

'What was he like?'

'I hardly spoke to him – just pleasantries really. But he was kind to us young officers. Took an interest. Benign.'

'He must have had a bit of steel in him though, if he was such a success in the war.'

'Oh yes,' I said. 'You could definitely sense that. He wasn't a man to cross.'

***

I had a few other things on for the next couple of days; not least Kate's forty-third birthday (drinks for around fifty of Leicestershire's great and good), so it wasn't until Tuesday that I sat down at my study desk and stared balefully at the three boxes on the corner.

After a moment's reflection I rang Charlie Manning, who picked up immediately.

'Ah, the author,' he said ironically. 'Persuasive, isn't he?'

'Always was,' I replied, confirming that I was on the hook.

'He gave me a whole lot of stuff from his father, and I'm going to digest that, which is apparently more than he's ever done. But I expect it'll be pretty personal. I need a wider perspective. Any ideas?'

Charlie paused for a moment.

'Well, I should start with Billy Mullins's history,' he said.

21

'I know it's reckoned to be pretty thin on D-Day and beyond, but it'll give you the basic chronology. You can build out from there.'

'Only one problem,' I replied.

'I know, you haven't got one,' sighed Charlie. 'Disgraceful. There are plenty knocking around here in Home Headquarters. I'll drop one in the post this evening.'

'Thanks,' I said. 'That'll definitely be useful. But what I'd really like to do is reach some of the old and bold who were there. To add a bit of colour, get a few anecdotes – that sort of thing. How would I do it?'

There was another pause on the end of the line.

'You know, I went to the funeral of my Uncle Tim a couple of months ago,' mused Charlie. 'Battle of Britain pilot. I spoke to a couple of his old Squadron chums afterwards. As one of them said, "The trouble with being one of 'the Few' is that we get fewer every year". It'll be the same here. It's a bloody long time ago.'

'Yes, but there must be a few still around from those days. Let's say you were twenty-five in 1945. Born 1920. So you'd be a sprightly eighty-five now. That's perfectly possible. And plenty of people will have written home. There should be some letters.'

'Well, we could always put something on the website,' said Charlie, portentously.

I smiled to myself. You've got to remember that this was nearly twenty years ago, and websites weren't such everyday things as they are now. I knew that Charlie had been laboriously supervising the construction of one on behalf of the Regiment, and that it had been launched with much fanfare two or three months previously. If truth be told it was pretty clunky, even for 2005, but it was very much Charlie's baby.

'Good idea,' I said, tactfully. 'Though I'm not sure how many eighty-five year olds spend their time on websites.'

'They need to get with it, then. This is the twenty-first century,' sniffed Charlie, who in some respects was barely out of the nineteenth.

'Anything else?' I probed.

I could sense Charlie cogitating on the other end of the line.

'Regimental journal – that comes out in about a month. Goes out each year to pretty much everyone who ever served, provided they're signed up for a five-quid direct debit. What about putting something in that? Timing's good. Copy deadline is Friday.'

'Definitely. I'll email something over for inclusion. You are on email, Charlie?' I said, teasingly.

'Indeed I am,' he said, defensively. 'Isn't everyone?'

I could think of a few people, but let it pass. 'OK,' I said. 'And I'll include something for the website too. It'll be interesting to see which does best.'

'Yes, won't it?' replied Charlie. 'I have faith in technology!'

But it was a thin veneer of confidence.

'I'm more of a Luddite,' I replied, twisting the knife gently. 'Please don't forget to post Billy's history.'

CHAPTER THREE

harlie was as good as his word, and the Mullins history arrived in the post a couple of days later. It was one of those 1950s editions which had once had an illustrated flysheet, long since gone, so now it was a bare, faded red hardback about two inches thick.

I opened it at random, taking in the yellowing paper. Though obviously old it was in good condition, well-illustrated with photos and maps, and would certainly serve my purpose. I turned the book over to look at its spine.

Armour in Battle: Prince Rupert's Horse, 1939–1945, it read, in gold text. Beneath that, in smaller font, was the name of the author: '*Billy Mullins MC.*'

I sat down with a cup of coffee. My intention was simply to skim through the book so I could assess the inadequacy of its coverage of the later war years relative to those where Billy had been personally present, but inevitably I got sucked into simply reading it. Somehow it was rather more interesting this time around than it had been a generation ago, when

I'd simply been swotting to forestall any probing of my inadequate regimental knowledge by the Adjutant.

Now, you can skip the rest of this chapter if you want, but I'm not going to drown you in military detail: stick with it and you'll have a much better understanding of the Regiment's situation in 1944.

Billy was a talented writer, and having known him in later life I could clearly sense his voice and manner in his prose: descriptive; informed; and never too serious, despite the frequent grimness of events. Where he could, he brought situations to life with anecdotes which told the reader far more about the reality of war than any number of academic treatises would have done.

I was quickly reminded what a harsh reality the Regiment's baptism of fire had been. It had only been mechanised in 1936, and when its reservists (those who had left in the last few years) were recalled in 1939 very few of them had any technical training: they were horsed cavalrymen. The officers likewise: most came from prosperous rural backgrounds, and had learned to ride at an early age, but with the exception of two wealthy young subalterns (one had his own aeroplane, the other was an amateur racing driver), mechanical knowledge was sorely lacking.

The Regiment's conversion training on Salisbury Plain in 1937 had been conducted with a mixed bag of obsolete tanks, fitted with inadequate numbers of dated and unreliable radios. The 1938 training season had been worse; many of the original tanks having been withdrawn to be spread around the rapidly expanding Army. Assigned that year to the fledgling 1st Armoured Division, there was only one opportunity for the Regiment to train with integrated artillery, engineers and signals, all equally newly arrived and inadequately equipped. It had not gone well.

Still incomplete, the Division had not gone to France with the British Expeditionary Force on the outbreak of war. On 6 May 1940 the first of its three Brigades, of which Rupert's was a part, had been put on ten days' notice to move, and began assimilating all sorts of tanks, many of them unfamiliar types in bad condition.

The intention was to resolve all this on arrival in France before being committed to action, but by the time the Regiment arrived in Cherbourg, still deficient in much basic equipment, the campaign was already lost.

As the BEF evacuated through Dunkirk, Rupert's and the rest of its parent Brigade were committed piecemeal to supporting the French Army along the line of the Somme River in a forlorn attempt to stem the Nazi tide.

Billy was frank about what followed, apologising for an 'incoherent account' of a chaotic period, during which he had been a Troop Leader in C Squadron. His fragmented vignettes gave a good impression of how hopeless it had all been. One of his tanks had gone into action with no gunsights, reliant on salvaging them from the first of its companions to be knocked out.

I sat up at one point, when Captain Giles Montagnon, then Regimental Signals Officer, made a characteristically competent debut: the French having ordered an attack with wholly insufficient time for preparation, he issued frequencies and codes 'as for the last Regimental exercise at Wimborne' – which fortunately he still had. The attack failed anyway.

Evacuation was ordered on 15 June, and what few

tanks remained in serviceable condition were carefully entrained at Le Mans for Cherbourg, never to be seen again. The manpower of the Regiment was taken on board badly overcrowded merchant shipping at Brest, arriving back in Plymouth late on 17 June. Some of them survived the dreadful sinking of SS *Lancastria* off St Nazaire, with over 4000 dead.

The campaign in France cost the Regiment three officers and fourteen soldiers killed; two officers (including the Commanding Officer, Lieutenant Colonel Henry Hammond) and seventeen soldiers wounded, and a total of twenty all ranks missing believed captured.

It had not been a good start – but then it had not been a good start for anyone wearing a British uniform; bit-part players in a contest between the much larger German and French armies.

I made myself another cup of coffee, and read on.

The rest of 1940 had been a matter of re-equipping with whatever was available as invasion loomed. Once the immediate emergency had receded over winter this could be done in rather more organised fashion, and by June 1941 the Regiment was reasonably well equipped and adequately trained, as was its parent 1st Armoured Division.

In August the Division was warned for overseas service in a month's time; destination unknown.

But the cookhouse rumour of the time had been a strong one.

As ever, it was right. Egypt.

***

'How are you getting on?' said Kate, sweeping in with a fresh cup of coffee a few minutes later, and deftly collecting the old one.

'I'm in November 1941,' I replied, ignoring a wry glance which implied that I probably belonged there. 'Different world. How long do you think it took the Regiment to reach North Africa?'

I could tell that Kate wasn't really interested, but she hazarded a guess to humour me. 'A month?'

'Ten weeks,' I replied, triumphantly. 'Of course, they had to go round the Cape. Far too dangerous through the Med.'

'Not much fun, I expect.'

'Actually they quite enjoyed it. Listen to this,' I said, and began reading aloud. '"Apart from the blackout, the lurking danger of enemy submarines and the lack of female company, it could have been a wonderful cruise."'

Kate sighed tolerantly, and tossed her shoulder-length brown hair.

'I think you'll find that's called irony,' she said over her shoulder, and beat a retreat back to the kitchen, where it was still 2005.

I read on easily through Billy's light prose, and amongst the moveable cast of characters kept an eye out for appearances by Giles Montagnon, who was clearly going to play a key part when it came to 1944 and beyond. A supposedly talented navigator, he made an early entrance when sent back to guide the Regiment's lost supply echelon forward during the long move to the front: it had paused after disembarkation only to collect its new tanks, with everyone learning the ways of the desert as they went.

Slightly off track on the return trip, he had come across a

minefield fence, with a couple of Guardsmen on sentry duty by a gap in the wire.

'How very fortunate,' Giles had said, anecdotally. 'Another few yards and we would all have been in a minefield.'

'On the contrary, sir,' replied one of the Guardsmen. 'Another few yards and you will be out of one.'

The first serious desert fighting in which the Regiment was involved had taken place in January 1942, and together with the rest of the Eighth Army it had been forced into a confused retreat, hampered by lack of supplies and the poor mechanical reliability of its Crusader tanks.

By the end of that period, and for reasons not made apparent in the text but probably due to casualties, Giles had moved from Command Troop, where he had been responsible for regimental communications, to become Second in Command of C Squadron, under Major Sandy Lucas-Smith, a celebrated pre-war horseman who had twice won the Grand Military at Sandown. I surmised that he was probably not an enthusiastic exponent of the Regiment's mechanisation.

I was skimming through by now, knowing the story of the Desert War well.

Billy led the reader lightly through the Gazala defeat, the retreat to Alamein, the defensive battle of Alam Halfa, and the re-equipment of most of the Regiment thereafter with much improved Sherman tanks, to everyone's great relief. From my perspective, the fact that Billy had been a Troop Leader in C Squadron was an added benefit, as most of the anecdotes which enlivened his tale came from that perspective. All the while I kept an eye on Giles, for whose calmness under pressure Billy clearly had a great deal of admiration. There was rather less said about Sandy Lucas-Smith, and I sensed that this omission was probably meaningful.

In October 1942 the Regiment took part in Montgomery's great offensive at El Alamein, where (like most of the armoured Regiments) it suffered severely. Part-way through, Sandy Lucas-Smith was 'evacuated' – reason not given.

Giles was promoted to replace him as C Squadron Leader, directly commanding (when at full strength, which was seldom) nineteen tanks and their supporting supply vehicles. He was thirty years old.

***

Monty has received much criticism from armchair generals for being too slow to pursue his defeated enemies after Alamein, but Billy's account made it plain that armoured Regiments like Rupert's simply outran their supplies in torrential rain (and consequent mud): its sixty-odd tanks had a voracious appetite for fuel, spares and ammunition, as did their crews for food and water. With logistic support concentrated elsewhere, Rupert's had gone into reserve for a while, and during this time news of decorations awarded earlier in the campaign came through.

To nobody's great surprise, one of four Military Crosses went to Giles, though he didn't receive it till later. Another, though he was too modest to say so, had gone to Billy.

Eventually – Tunisia, and the link-up in early 1943 with First Army and the Americans, who had landed in Algeria in November the previous year. By March the Germans and their Italian allies had been pushed back into a tight perimeter around Tunis, and in May some 250,000 of them had surrendered.

But not before Billy's active service career had come to an abrupt end.

It was phrased in the third person, and with typical modesty. 'On the 13th of April Lieutenant Mullins was seriously wounded by shellfire whilst temporarily dismounted from his tank to answer a call of nature.'

Thus the story of the Regiment's service in World War Two as written by an eyewitness was over.

After assurances that it would not be sent home to participate in the invasion of the Continent which everyone knew was coming because of 'shipping constraints', it came as a great surprise after several weeks kicking its heels for the Regiment to receive orders to embark at Alexandria for passage back to the United Kingdom.

Monty, newly appointed to command ground forces during the invasion, wanted to leaven the untried troops in England with some hard-won experience. 'Shipping constraints' were overcome.

***

As only the Army could do, no sooner had it recovered Rupert's to the UK in November 1943 on account of the Regiment's supposed expertise in tank warfare than it promoted the much-loved and highly experienced Henry Hammond to become a Deputy Brigade Commander.

Appointed in his stead was a regular cavalryman from another Regiment. This officer had spent the entire period since 1939 on the Staff in the War Office, and was now deemed to require 'command experience' in the field for the purposes of his career.

Billy mentioned him only occasionally by name in his history, and though not present himself made it abundantly clear that this was not a successful appointment. Ambrose Wolfram ('The Wolf') took one look at his returning desert warriors (who admittedly fostered a somewhat relaxed attitude to dress), and instantly decided that what they needed above all else was smartening up. He would have done much better to focus on spreading the practical knowledge of his veterans amongst the many new officers and soldiers who were posted into the Regiment – and indeed on picking their brains himself.

But he seemingly lacked the confidence to lean on his more experienced subordinates.

The result, as D-Day approached, was by inference (although never explicitly stated by Billy) an unhappy and febrile unit, with little confidence in its Commanding Officer, a dismissive approach to learning anything new, and an unhealthy 'why us again?' mindset amongst many of its experienced Non-Commissioned Officers – the backbone of any Regiment.

In this state it deployed to Normandy on 8 June 1944 (D+2), with Giles Montagnon still C Squadron Leader. By D+5 'The Wolf' was dead, killed by a sniper during a reckless recce in close country, probably (Billy speculated) because he had no idea what else to do when things didn't go according to plan.

As Billy trenchantly observed – 'in war; they never do.'

Major Bobby Lomax, the Second in Command, himself new to combat, took over to surprisingly good effect in the immediate aftermath. But as he was the first to tell the Brigade Commander subsequently, he lacked experience of leading men in battle, and the confidence of the troops that came with it.

Giles Montagnon was that man, and although theoretically senior, Bobby would happily serve under him.

So that's what happened. It was also almost the last colourful episode in Billy's regimental history, no doubt because he had heard the circumstances first hand from Bobby, who was his cousin.

Thereafter it was just a mass of dates, place names and casualties, with little underpinning detail.

During the next ten months the young Commanding Officer of Prince Rupert's Horse acquired two Distinguished Service Orders, a Mention in Despatches, and a US Silver Star to add to the Military Cross he had earned in the desert.

But the reader was left with very little impression of how he had done so.

CHAPTER FOUR

'So?' said Kate, once I had emerged bleary-eyed from my study, and joined her in the kitchen.

'They're right,' I replied. 'It's pretty well colourless throughout the time Jazzer's father was in command – and even before that, once the Regiment arrived back from Africa. There's the odd glimmer, where Billy obviously spoke to somebody who was there, but you can sense his lack of interest once he's no longer around himself. It's dull. Certainly compared to the earlier stuff.'

Kate turned off the kitchen radio, which was rare. I sensed genuine interest.

'Does that mean you'll have to start from scratch?'

'As good as,' I replied. 'Billy's given me the basic chronology, which is useful. But I've got to bring it all to life.'

'How?'

I shrugged.

'Anecdote. Personal experience. Retrospective opinion. Detail. Context. There are still a fair few old boys around from those days, though they were mostly pretty junior at the time. Even many who aren't still with us will have written letters home, or family memoirs. I've got an appeal for anything like that going into the regimental journal, which will come out next month. And our museum curator in Newark has promised Charlie that he'll push something out too. They've got a very well-informed 'Friends of Prince Rupert's Horse' mailing list, apparently.'

'It'll take some time for all that to produce anything worthwhile, surely?' said Kate, dubiously.

'True,' I replied. 'But whilst I'm waiting I've got all that stuff Jazzer gave me to wade through.'

'Won't that be fun for you?' said my darling wife lightly, as if speaking to a ten-year-old. Though she may even have meant it; I remember thinking that at the time.

Even after thirteen years of marriage, I could never tell with her.

***

Box One

The next day I prevaricated: read the papers; walked the dogs; answered some wholly unimportant mail. Kate was out somewhere, or I wouldn't have got away with it. But after I'd raided the fridge for lunch, I was flat out of excuses.

I made myself a coffee, and reluctantly retired to my study, where Jazzer's boxes were awaiting me. They looked reproachful. So did my two spaniels, Milo and Rosie, settling down reluctantly at my feet after their walk.

My desk is an old Georgian one, inherited from my

father, though now looking rather incongruous with a big white computer on top of it. I did a little unenthusiastic tidying, because that's always necessary in my case, with several books needing to be returned to the shelves. Then with a sigh I pulled the nearest box over, having decided over lunch that a relatively painless way to start would be an audit of what I'd actually got.

When I opened it, I saw some handwritten labelling on the inside of the top flap: 'Desert 1942–43'. I hadn't expected organised cataloguing. Curious, I got up to look at the other two boxes. The first of these said 'Early Days and 1939–41' in the same place. The final box was labelled 'North West Europe 1944–45'. Given the intended focus of my new history I was glad to see that this box contained considerably more material than the others.

I thought I'd better proceed chronologically, so started with 'Early Days'.

There wasn't a huge amount in this first box, but what there was revealed quite a lot about Giles.

I began with several old photos of varying sizes, all black and white of course. There were three piles, each loosely bound together with old brown rubber bands: some on cardboard backings, some loose. Many had the serrated white edges so typical of the period. After removing the rubber bands, I spread the first pile out on the large table a few feet from the desk.

Easily the biggest photo was what had been the bottom one. It was an Uppingham School house photograph: The Hall; 1930. Front and centre of the fifty or so stern-looking teenagers in their cricket blazers was G. Montagnon (House Captain); sitting alongside the housemaster, who gave every appearance of deference to him.

Early evidence of leadership abilities, it seemed.

Giles was obviously a sporting gladiator. I leafed briefly through pictures of him in rugby and cricket attire, once flourishing some grandiose cup. There were random pictures of him with horses, and in the shooting field – also in evening dress, arm in arm with some young girl; both teenagers, and looking uncharacteristically solemn.

And then suddenly there he was in uniform, dressed as a private soldier: 'Royal Military Academy Sandhurst – Champion Platoon, 1932'.

There were twenty-eight eager young faces in the photograph. In rough woollen battledress, they flanked their Captain instructor, who was in a tailored officer service uniform. He looked old and tired by comparison, and sported a string of First World War medals. Probably almost forty – bloody ancient for a job like that, I reflected.

Giles was top right in the picture, grinning happily. It looked as if soldiering suited him.

I was about to set the photo aside when I noticed that ten of the figures had a tiny cross inked in next to their names. It needed no explanation.

Thoughtfully I turned to the next picture – Giles as a Second Lieutenant, wearing the Number One dress uniform of Prince Rupert's Horse. It was a formal commissioning picture, dated 7 December 1932. The uniform seemed much as it had when I'd been commissioned myself nearly fifty years later. He looked very young.

The Regiment was still horsed cavalry at this time, as became apparent in the next few photos, taken at Tidworth, with young officers exercising in the indoor riding school under the eagle eye of the veteran Riding Master. One of them showed Giles laughing in the dirt, presumably after an involuntary dismount. The Riding Master looked on with stern disapproval.

There were a few more carefree photos: mess dinners; hunt balls; dogs; stables; revolver practice; sword drill. Nothing whatever though of Giles's home life though, I noted.

And then, suddenly, it was 1936. The Regiment's twenty or so officers, Giles amongst them (and now a full Lieutenant) posed grimly on and around a cruiser tank of indeterminate vintage: an unfamiliar monster.

The photo's caption contained only one word. 'Mechanisation.' Dread moment for all cavalry Regiments, though they must have known it was inevitable – indeed well overdue.

The second pile, which was smaller, continued on chronologically. Tanks; all sorts of weird and wonderful types, often under repair – and mostly it seemed on Salisbury Plain, which I recognised had not changed greatly by the time of my own service many years later. This was no doubt the conversion training of 1937, to which Billy's history had referred.

There was a stray photo of Giles in mess dress, with a young woman on his arm – possibly the one who had appeared earlier, though on checking I couldn't be sure.

The third pile, smaller still, contained only a dozen or so photos. They were clearly taken during the brief, inglorious French campaign of 1940. There were a couple of the embarkation, one or two of the Regiment (or part of it) retraining and in leaguer in France, and little else other than some very sombre and grimy individuals pictured on a crowded ship home.

Giles was apparently the photographer. He appeared in only one shot, together with a fellow officer: an early selfie. Both were attempting to smile, but their exhaustion was obvious. With a start I recognised a very young Billy Mullins as the other party.

There were a few other bits and pieces in the box; nothing spectacular, though I was pleased to see a set of much-thumbed signals instructions, which I equated with the recycled ones from the Wimborne exercise to which Billy had referred in his history. There were a couple of maps too, but unmarked, and thus not very informative. I spread everything out on the table.

Nowhere was there any commentary by Giles on events. But this mattered little to me, since 1940 was not my intended focus.

***

Box Two

As I opened 'The Desert' my focus went up a notch, since I was getting closer to my period of interest.

This time, instead of the piles of photos held together by rubber bands, I was pleased to see an actual album. It had a black, faded cover. As I vaguely thumbed through it I immediately saw that the photos had not been glued in, but were held in place by those little corner holders so typical of the period.

Inevitably a few of the pictures had come loose. I put these carefully to one side on the table, keeping them separate from the contents of the first box.

Before I started on a proper review of the album I spent ten minutes with Billy's history, just to remind myself of the sequence of events. And indeed there was a significant correlation.

The early photographs were taken on board a troopship, the SS *Masonic* – her name could plainly be seen on the lifeboats, and there was a general view of her alongside the quay, presumably at Southampton. Thereafter there were indeed photos that might have been taken on a cruise, as Billy said, though there was also a sequence picturing monstrous waves, labelled simply 'Biscay.'

Giles had captioned many of the photos, but annoyingly only as a reminder to himself – thus when picturing people he used only Christian names, or nicknames. But there was a useful 'Order of Battle on Arrival in Africa' annex in Billy's history, and I was soon able to match most of the names to their pictures.

I noted in particular Sandy, whom I knew would later become Giles's Squadron Leader. He looked very much a conventional member of the landed gentry of the period, with blond, slicked-down hair centrally parted, and a small moustache. Unlike most of the other officers, he was not smiling in the picture Giles had taken of him onboard ship, leaning against the rail. I fancied I recognised the type from my own service: rank conscious, and not prepared to unwind with his juniors. It was seldom a good sign.

On arrival at Cape Town there were a few general tourist-type pictures, no doubt taken during a brief period of leave, and then the scene shifted abruptly to the desert, without seemingly taking in Alexandria, or the rear areas of Eighth Army. After this the photos were disappointingly similar, probably due to the constraints of time, and Giles's busy role. I noted a few posed photos of his Command Troop, and of Regimental Headquarters deployed in the desert, no doubt all taken before any serious action had taken place.

Thereafter there were a lot of views of tanks: bombing up; refuelling; broken down; charging across the desert; and in some cases, knocked out. Initially they were Crusaders, but these faded away as more modern and reliable types became available. The first appearance of Shermans was heralded by a close-up of one of these much-improved tanks with a delighted crew. The picture was labelled 'Sherman – at last!'

Occasionally enemy equipment featured: knocked-out tanks and transport, or sometimes a dreaded 88 mm anti-tank gun: a type which caused the Regiment much grief. A few Italian and German prisoners made cameo appearances, many of them looking surprisingly cheerful.

Interspersed were the personalities, with Christian names as before. There was a small cairn with the sad little caption: 'Grave of Robin and his crew', which I cross-referenced back to Billy's history: Second Lieutenant The Honourable Robin Blane of C Squadron had been killed during the Gazala battles on the 27 May 1942. There had been no survivors when his tank blew up. By then Giles was Second in Command of that Squadron, and another photo showed him in the turret of his Sherman, which sported a prominent circle marking (A Squadron would have had triangles, and B Squadron squares: it was the same in my day, when I had always been a C Squadron man, and probably still is).

There was a striking photo taken at dusk, presumably from that same turret, with a line of tanks ahead, and the flashes of artillery in the distance. It was labelled 'Moon

Track.' This I knew from a fine Terence Cuneo painting in the officers' mess (perhaps taken from that very photograph) was the Regiment moving up for Alamein.

Next was a picture of Giles with his tank crew, sporting Major's rank insignia. All of them were grinning broadly. 'Squadron Leader', said the caption. There was no hint of what had happened to his predecessor.

I skimmed pretty quickly through the rest of the album. The pursuit (bogged down), the period in reserve, and the move forward to Tunisia were all documented.

The surrender came surprisingly quickly, with photos of massed prisoners, together with captured equipment, including one of the formidable new Tiger tanks. Cheerful members of C Squadron swarmed over the great beast, which had a large 'Rupert's' flag draped from its bazooka plates.

The album ended with a smiling Giles sporting his Military Cross, presumably just after being awarded it. There was no citation, but I was confident I would be able to track that down.

I looked at what else was in the box. An Afrika Korps forage cap was obviously a souvenir. Beyond that were a stack of letters, tied up with a faded orange ribbon. There were at least fifty; it was the pile I had picked up at Jazzer's house.

I flicked through them briefly. They were all in the same fine hand. A woman's hand.

I didn't think they would be relevant, nor did I want to pry. I put them on the table, next to the rest of the contents of the box, intending to sample them later.

***

Box Three

Of course, the third box was for me the main event, and it contained gratifyingly more than the others. Giles appeared to have made at least some attempt to organise the contents. There was another photo album, which I put aside for the moment, and then a succession of orange folders.

I picked out one of these at random.

It appeared to catalogue a specific action, which had taken place on 16 July 1944. There was a Divisional Operation Order (Operation Ascot); a creased map; a notebook containing some hasty scribbles in the traditional 'Orders' sequence (still in use I believe); a map crudely marked with chinagraph symbols – I surmised the one Giles had used on the day – and a written card describing the event using military abbreviations, most of which were familiar to me. I recognised his handwriting from the photograph captions in the earlier albums.

I could see from the abbreviations that the Regiment was part of 8 Independent Armoured Brigade. The role of this Brigade in 'Ascot' was to provide tank support to an Infantry Division, which lacked inherent armour.

I reflected on this as a former tank officer: quite a frustrating role for Giles. All his Squadrons were parcelled out to infantry battalions, leaving him with nothing under his direct command. On balance, most tank men would have preferred the exploitation/pursuit role of the armoured divisions rather than the hard grind of breaking through enemy defences with the infantry. Giles's one-word verdict on a certain famous armoured division's performance after 'Ascot' was withering: 'sticky'.

Placing the folder on the table, I took up another. It was

much the same. There were around thirty of them, which matched well with Billy's overall chronology, so in due course I'd have a solid basis for my descriptions of those actions. No doubt a few of the photos would be useful, but the folders lacked the personal detail I was seeking.

I'd need to wait for the results of my appeal for that.

CHAPTER FIVE

I was still scanning through the photo album when Kate returned from wherever she'd been. I heard her call out cheerfully from the kitchen, asking if I wanted a cup of tea. Only one answer to that of course.

She paused briefly on seeing the detritus spread out across the table when she came through, and then handed me my mug.

'Research under way, I see.'

'Well, not really – not yet,' I replied. 'I'm just taking stock of what I've got.'

She nodded in acknowledgement, and wandered unhurriedly around the table looking at the assorted items. I kept half an eye on her as I returned to my album, and we browsed in companionable silence.

After a couple of minutes I sensed her pause, and looked up.

'What are these?' she said. She was holding the letters from the second box.

'Letters to Giles,' I replied. 'They were in the desert box. From some woman I think. I haven't looked at them yet.'

Kate leafed through them curiously.

'Would you mind if I did?' she asked, looking up with that sudden glance I knew so well.

'Not at all,' I replied, slightly surprised. 'Just make sure they go back where you found them.'

She smiled at me gratefully, and retreated to the kitchen. She did everything around the island there; it doubled as her desk.

I started reading more of the orange files. Kate was gone for nearly half an hour, and then stuck her head round the door.

'What was Giles's wife called?' she said.

'Is,' I said. 'She's still alive. Rowena, I think.'

Kate nodded with satisfaction, and waved one of the letters at me. 'These are from Rowena.'

She turned on her heel, and went back to the kitchen. Five minutes later she was back.

'When did they marry?' she asked.

I sighed, dug an old 'Army List' off one of the shelves behind me, and consulted it briefly.

'Saturday 4th of March 1950,' I said, snapping it shut. 'Why?'

Kate smiled enigmatically, and resumed her casual examination of the items on the table. She seemed to be looking for something specific from the third box.

Then she stopped.

'Hmm,' she said mysteriously, knowing I'd be unable to resist following up.

'What?' I asked, wearily.

46

'Minor mystery,' she said. 'You write dozens of letters to a man who's fighting in the desert. Then he comes home for a few months, and goes off again to fight in France after D-Day. You don't write to him at all there. Then, five years after the war, you marry him. Odd, isn't it?'

'Well,' I said, a little dubiously. 'If you put it like that, yes. But her letters probably just got lost, or he was too busy fighting in France to keep them. I don't think it means much.'

Kate raised her eyebrows. I never cease to be amazed at the mass of different emotions that woman can convey by such a simple act: it's one of her many unique qualities.

Unless I was much mistaken, this time it was a carefully calibrated mix of 'oh really'; 'I know better;' and 'foolish boy.'

She retired again to the kitchen with a suitably mysterious smile, and no doubt to the letters.

***

The journal had yet to appear, but Charlie had put my appeal for information up on his much-vaunted website, and within days the responses began to dribble in.

Mostly they were pretty thin gruel – just people who had served in the Regiment at a junior level, or their descendants, with the odd photo or unlikely anecdote. But nothing that would provide the colour and insight that I sought. After about a week I became rather despondent about it.

Then I got a good old-fashioned letter, written on headed notepaper. It was quite short, but intrigued me immediately.

Dear Mr Mallory,
    This is a response to your recent appeal for information.

I am the daughter of Celia Hart (nee Sweetman), sister of Lieutenant Michael Sweetman, who was an officer in Prince Rupert's Horse. As I am sure the records will show (and you may already be aware), my uncle was killed whilst serving in Germany on the 24th of March 1945. He was 24.

Both my grandparents then being dead, some of his private effects thereafter reached my mother, amongst them letters which you may find interesting. My mother (now deceased) also received a few letters directly from him, and I have those too. She was only 16 when her brother died.

I would be very pleased to show you this material, and (if you are sufficiently interested) to loan it to you whilst you write your history.

Yours sincerely,
Georgina Hart

I paused for thought. Unmarried, it seemed: she still carried her original surname. Probably born sometime between the mid-fifties and the mid-sixties, judging by her mother's age in 1944. Split the difference: perhaps forty-five now?

The address on the headed paper was near a village outside Towcester, not that far away. On impulse I dialled the number given. It rang only twice before being picked up.

'Hello?' said a friendly female voice: rather husky.

'Georgina Hart?' I said.

'Yes – that's me,' she replied. She didn't seem at all defensive or suspicious, as many people are when they receive unsolicited calls.

'This is Dominic Mallory. You wrote to me about your uncle's letters.'

48

'That's very quick of you: I only posted my note yesterday.'

'Well – no point in hanging about,' I replied briskly. 'I'd certainly like to see that material if the offer still stands.'

'Of course,' she said, sounding pleased. 'How shall we—?'

'I suggest you let me buy you lunch,' I said, cutting her off. 'The very least I can do.'

'Well, that's very good of you,' she replied, uncertainly. 'When?'

'Whenever best suits you.'

After a bit of to and fro we agreed to meet on the following Wednesday, at a pub called The Folly near Towcester racecourse, which she recommended and agreed to book.

'How will I recognise you?' she said lightly, after this exchange.

I thought for a moment.

'Tell you what,' I said. 'I've got a particularly fetching green jacket that my wife never allows me to wear. It'll give me a good excuse.'

She laughed. 'Green jacket, twelve-thirty. See you then.'

'Yes – until then.'

I put the phone down in high good humour. I liked the sound of Georgina Hart.

***

The following day I was booked in to see Charlie Manning at Home Headquarters in Newark, which was close to the Regimental Museum. He had told me that between them they held quite a bit of material which would probably be of interest to my project. I took along a photocopy of Georgina's letter which they could add to their file, plus ones of the other assorted bits and pieces I had been sent following my post on the website.

Whilst I waited in the foyer to be admitted through the secure door I admired a large photo of the then Prince Charles wearing his regimental tie and smiling broadly, taken perhaps twenty years before. Having been raised in Newark by the Royalists in the Civil War, with inordinately large portraits of Charles the First and his nephew Prince Rupert dominating the officers' mess, we have always made the future Charles the Third very welcome – and though he has yet to visit as sovereign, I am sure we still will. We like to think that he enjoys coming to us more than other Regiments of which he is Colonel in Chief (some of which, if old enough, have dubious Parliamentarian origins) – and to make the point, as quasi-cavaliers, officers in Rupert's of my vintage always wore their hair as long as the Regiment's current Brigade Commander would tolerate. All a bit of a game, especially if he happened to be a Guardsman.

The door opened, and I was greeted by the Admin Officer, Amy Moss, a spinster of indeterminate vintage who had been at Home Headquarters for as long as anyone could remember. She had an encyclopaedic knowledge of all former regimental officers. In her world they retained their rank in perpetuity – thus I was of course 'Captain Mallory'. Lieutenants and Second Lieutenants were mere 'Misters'. Even former cabinet ministers and peers of the realm were no exception to this rule. On one celebrated occasion a Duke who had once spent three years with us when he was a mere Marquis had allegedly once been called 'Mr Grace' when Amy had got mildly confused.

Having navigated Amy and exchanged a few words on

the way in with the Finance Manager, Anvi Kumar, another longstanding regimental servant, I had a coffee with Charlie and his Assistant Regimental Secretary. He was another retired Officer, Captain Sam Lane.

Sam had been a promising Lance Corporal back in my day, fortunately in C Squadron, so I knew him vaguely, and even then he had stood out as a man to watch. Now he was an example of that relatively rare and much respected phenomenon, the 'Late Entry' Officer, commissioned from the ranks after long, exemplary and loyal service. A former Regimental Sergeant Major, and still crop-headed, post commissioning he had held the post of Technical Quartermaster for a brief period before retirement and assumption of the role as Charlie's assistant a couple of years before. Aside from still being extremely fit, he was well versed in regimental history: though Charlie cheerily told me that 'we've got some things ready for you,' I was under no illusions as to who had done the legwork: Sam even winked at me as Charlie said it.

Bounding up two steps at a time, Sam led me upstairs, where the material he thought I might be interested in had been laid out on a table in the conference room. I paused to take it in.

'So what have you got for me, Sam?' I said, after a moment's reflection.

Sam needed no second bidding.

'Well, let's start with the obvious – pictures,' he said. 'This is pretty unusual.'

There were two albums on the table, nearly identical. He picked up one of this pair, and handed it to me. Curious, I opened it, whilst Sam looked on expectantly.

The inside cover had an ornately styled caption: 'Officers at Regimental Duty with Prince Rupert's Horse – 1 June 1944.'

I looked up at Sam. 'A few days before D-Day.'

He nodded. 'Those men led the Regiment into battle. Take a look.'

I leafed through the album. They were all upper body shots, in a variety of poses, and organised according to roles held at the time. Under 'Regimental Headquarters' much the largest photo was captioned 'Commanding Officer – Lieutenant Colonel Ambrose Wolfram.'

'Dead a few days later,' said Sam, seeing where my attention lay. 'No bad thing, by all accounts.'

I looked up at him, surprised at his bluntness. He met my gaze steadily.

'Social soldier.'

It was a damning verdict. I looked back at the immaculately turned out, unsmiling figure with the receding chin, and couldn't help concluding that Sam was probably right – fixated with turnout and smartness rather than the realities of war.

My gaze wandered briefly over the others in Regimental Headquarters, with their smaller pictures, noting in particular the cheery, chubby face of the Second in Command, Major Robert Lomax, clutching a steaming mug in some wooded glade.

I turned over to A Squadron, and gave the pictures brief scrutiny. I was about to turn over when I noted a small photo bottom-left on the same page. '1st Troop Leader – Lieutenant Michael Sweetman,' it said. With the call to Georgina Hart fresh in my mind I looked at the figure curiously: good looking, certainly, with a shock of dark curly hair. He was sitting on a chair outside a tent in shirtsleeves, caught in three-quarter profile, and appeared to be laughing with someone to his front who had been cropped out of the picture.

'Could I have a copy of this?' I said, turning to Sam. He raised his eyebrows in mild surprise, and I told him the reason.

'I'll get you a photocopy. We've got another copy of the album.' Sam clattered down the stairs.

Thereafter I simply leafed through, seeing that as expected, C Squadron Leader was 'Major Giles Montagnon MC.' The picture was not one I had seen before, and showed him caught unawares in his tank turret, with its C Squadron circle insignia. He was wearing headphones over his beret, and studying a map with deep concentration.

Once I had finished I picked up the album's twin. It was very much the same layout, only this time it was headed 'Officers at Regimental Duty with Prince Rupert's Horse – 10 May 1945.'

Two days after the German surrender. This time the Commanding Officer was 'Lieutenant Colonel Giles Montagnon, DSO and bar; MC.' In battledress with medal ribbons, and apparently in best parade order, it was a full-face shot; serious and strained. There was none of the exultation of victory.

I heard Sam come back into the room with my photocopy, which he handed over silently.

'Not much in common between that album and this one,' he said, as he replaced the 1944 version back on the table. 'I think you'll only find five people who appear in both. Including him, of course.'

I was surprised by the fondness in his voice, but shouldn't have been.

'Like father like son, then, you reckon?' I said, as my memory returned.

'Damn sure of it,' said Sam, who only a few years before had been Regimental Sergeant Major to another Lieutenant Colonel Montagnon in Kosovo.

***

I thought the next item Sam had laid out for me might be a bit of a goldmine.

It was a photocopy of the Regimental War Diary, dating from the day it had landed in Normandy, 8 June 1944, and with a few gaps (probably when the pressure was greatest) it ran through to the end of the war. Maintained by the Adjutant, Captain Alastair Gill, it was in effect a first draft of history – a day-by-day account of what the Regiment had done and what had befallen it, written at the time. Sometimes a day would be covered by a single sentence. For others the commentary was almost minute by minute.

But it was a false dawn. What rapidly became apparent was that Billy's history was in large measure simply a regurgitation of the War Diary in front of me, at times almost verbatim.

'Thank you; this will be useful,' I said, turning to Sam and attempting to hide my disappointment.

I put the photocopy in my briefcase, and turned to the next item which Sam handed me. It was a small black prayer book, with a faded gold cross on the front: much battered, and perhaps five inches by three. I looked at the flyleaf in curiosity, where there was what I thought was a dedication written in faded ink. On closer inspection it was simply the owner's name.

'Nicholas Carson' it read. 'Padre, PRH.'

It seemed somehow that the phrase had been written with pride.

'You know whose that is?' asked Sam.

I nodded. Anyone with any knowledge of Prince Rupert's Horse in the Second World War knew of Nick Carson: not many regimental padres had won the Military Cross. There was even a small painting of him in the officers' mess, with the ribbon on his tunic, looking terrifyingly young.

'Why have we got it?' I asked.

'He left it behind, I think. We tried to give it back to him many years ago. It seems he didn't want it.'

Sam shrugged: no accounting for the ways of men of the cloth, he implied.

'That's odd. I wonder why?'

'A gift to the Regiment, maybe. Why not ask him?'

'You mean he's still alive?' I said, surprised.

'I believe so. Not been in touch with anyone for years.'

'A recluse?'

'Seems to be. I don't know really.'

'Do you have an address?'

Sam sighed, and turned to a filing cabinet behind him: this was long before the days of computerised databases, at least in places like the Home Headquarters of distinguished old fighting Regiments. He took out a sheet from a file, and headed off downstairs again to his photocopier.

When Sam came back I looked at the data sheet he gave me. The space for the photo was blank. But there was an address near Oxford, plus a date of birth: 20 January 1920.

So he was eighty-five.

Sam saw the way my thoughts were drifting, and shook his head amiably.

'He won't see you,' he said.

'We'll see,' I said with a grin, handing the prayer book back to him. 'I'm very persuasive.'

CHAPTER SIX

Wednesday came around pretty quickly. Kate had been out for the morning, and I was making my way to the car for my trip to Towcester when she came bowling up the drive in her Volvo 4 x 4. I saw her grimace through the window as she drew level with me.

'You're not going out in public wearing that, surely?' she said sternly, as she got out of the car, though there was a hint of playfulness there somewhere. But as ever with her, I couldn't quite tell.

'Certainly am,' I said, flexing the sleeves of my green jacket. 'For recognition.'

'Recognition? Oh, your mystery lunch date.' She didn't sound that interested. 'What's she wearing? A golden tutu?'

'I'm certain she'll look perfectly delightful,' I said, as I opened my car door. 'Hoping so, anyway.'

Kate smiled, and locked her car. She blew me a quick kiss and turned to go inside.

'Tell me all about it later,' she said, over her shoulder,

and fluttered her hand in a 'goodbye' gesture. 'Hope it's useful.'

If truth be told I wasn't at all convinced it would be. But I had precious little else to go on at this early stage, so it was worth a punt, I reflected, as I set my satnav: they were pretty embryonic then. I enjoyed using it.

It was well under an hour's run, with very little traffic, and I drew up in the pub car park at twelve-twenty as intended, aiming to be settled once Georgina Hart arrived.

The Folly was delightful – clearly old, but comfortable, well patronised and tastefully decorated. I bought myself a pint of bitter and settled back comfortably at an outside table with a view of the car park, musing upon what my lunch companion would be like whilst idly perusing what seemed a very decent menu.

I didn't have long to wait; she arrived almost exactly on time in a Volkswagen Golf and made her way straight over to me, the green jacket having fulfilled its purpose.

In the few seconds before she reached me I took stock as I rose to my feet. Rather more petite than I'd expected (not more than five foot five); friendly, open smile; smart blue coat; black boots; well cut, dark, shoulder-length hair. Age – about what I'd expected. And attractive. Most definitely attractive.

'Dom Mallory,' I said, reaching out to shake her hand.

'Georgina. I'm so thrilled you're interested. Nice jacket!'

She was carrying a large envelope in addition to her handbag. I ushered her to her seat.

'First things first. Drink?'

She settled on a ginger beer, which I ordered from a passing waitress: I could see her sizing me up as I did so.

'So,' I said, without much originality once I had made the order. 'It's very good to meet you.'

'Well – let me show you,' said Georgina, taking out the contents of the envelope.

It wasn't a huge amount. There were two sets of letters, each with a couple of rubber bands around it – one looked marginally thicker than the other, but neither contained more than half a dozen envelopes.

I waited for her to explain.

'There's not much,' she said, apologetically, and looked up. Green eyes. 'But I thought they might add some of the colour you said you were seeking.'

'So what have we got?'

'Well,' she said theatrically as her drink arrived, whilst flashing me a conspiratorial glance. 'This first set is to Michael; he kept them: they're from his wife.'

'His wife? I thought he was only twenty-four?'

She shrugged and glanced up again, rather delightfully. 'Wartime.'

'And what do they say?'

'It's mainly just gossip; mundane day-to-day stuff. That's probably what he wanted to hear – something of his old life. There's not much about the war beyond "keep safe". She probably didn't know how to articulate that. Very young, of course.'

I picked up the pile curiously, and began to remove the rubber band. Georgina waved her hand airily.

'No need to read them now,' she said. 'Take them away.'

'Sure?'

She nodded, and indicated the second pile. 'And that second set is from him. To his sister, my mother.'

Again, I picked them up briefly. Only four letters.

'Can I take these as well?'

'Of course. They're rather touching. He's trying not to worry her: making it all sound like a big game. There are some good character sketches of his fellow officers which may interest you.'

I showed Georgina the photocopied picture of her uncle which I'd got from Home Headquarters, which she professed never to have seen before, and seemed delighted by, so I promised to send her a copy.

Then I put the photo and the two bundles of letters into the zip-up leather slip I'd brought with me, and turned my full attention to my companion. We ordered our food.

Like most men I always find it stimulating to talk to an attractive woman, even if one has no designs on her beyond sharing a decent meal – especially if she is an easy and amusing conversationalist, as Georgina most certainly was. I was already aware that she was single from her surname, though from a few cryptic hints she dropped it seemed that there might have been some long-term relationship in the past. She was happy to flirt harmlessly, and seemed to enjoy my company, which is always flattering.

I wondered what she did, and when it didn't crop up I eventually decided to ask her.

'Journalist,' she replied coolly. 'Freelance.'

***

Journalism is a fascinating profession if (like me) you enjoy writing.

Journalists – now that's another kettle of fish altogether.

I'd come across quite a few of them in my time, both

in the military and during my subsequent City career. My experience had been mixed. Some were dedicated pursuers of the truth (albeit often with a pre-conceived notion of it); others chased an angle that would give them an exclusive, even if it meant wilfully misinterpreting the facts in front of them. And I'd learnt that if you were (say) a soldier, or perhaps an executive in the City, some of the fourth estate would automatically default to a position of absolute scepticism about anything you had to say.

If not actually burnt by this experience I'd certainly been gently singed by it a couple of times, so I was immediately wary, reviewing our conversation up to that point.

But it all seemed pretty harmless, even when Georgina told me that she was an investigative journalist whenever she could find a story which was good enough to merit the extensive time this specialisation required. However, most of her time was actually spent on human interest articles – 'my bread and butter.'

'Safer too, no doubt?' I replied at this revelation.

Georgina considered the question seriously, though I'd asked it in a fairly flippant manner. She pouted in a rather distracting manner whilst she did so.

'Well, it can be a rough trade,' she said, after a few seconds' pause. 'If it's a worthwhile story then someone has a vested interest in hushing it up, or at least steering it in a certain direction.'

'Ever been genuinely scared?' I asked.

'Sure,' she said with a ready smile. 'I find it bloody terrifying ringing people up out of the blue – particularly if they've got an unsavoury reputation. It's actually much better to see them face to face: they're unlikely to be as blatantly rude as they might be on the phone, and you can judge the body language.'

Georgina was a natural raconteur, and told me about a few of her cases over the rest of the meal, both successful and otherwise. It was both amusing and informative.

After I'd paid, and as we made our way over to the car park together, I thanked her once again for taking the trouble to get in touch, and for agreeing to meet me.

'No problem; I enjoyed it very much,' she responded with a smile. 'Thank you for lunch.'

After a brief moment of hesitation she fished in her handbag, and handed me a card with her contact details. I had some of my business cards in my wallet, so returned the gesture.

'Well, I owe you a favour,' I said, as we shook hands rather awkwardly: though we'd got on notably well it was too soon for a kiss on the cheek.

'I'll hold you to that,' she replied, stepping back. 'Genuinely. If it looks like there's a story here, will you promise to let me know? A human interest angle?'

I considered this briefly. It might even help drum up interest in the book.

'Of course, that's the least I can do,' I replied. I didn't quite recognise the thought behind my agreement at the time, but I do now: I wanted a reason to see Georgina again, simply because I liked her.

And what possible harm could there be in her getting a story?

***

When I got home Kate was in the kitchen having tea with her good friend Amelia, with whom she was thick as thieves. I'd very clearly interrupted their gossip, but they looked gratifyingly pleased to see me all the same.

'So, how was it?' asked Kate. She'd obviously already explained the nature of my absence to Amelia.

'Very useful, actually,' I replied. 'She gave me some letters and things. Well worth the trip.'

'What was she like?'

'Nice.'

'Good looking?' asked my dear wife, offhandedly. I waved a hand airily in response.

'All right, I suppose…'

'She was good looking!' said Amelia, firmly. 'Honestly, men! Totally transparent in the face of totty.'

She undoubtedly had experience of exerting such allure herself, being six feet tall, slim and blonde. I smiled sheepishly, helped myself to a cuppa and sat down.

'She's a journalist actually. If I dig up anything intriguing, I'm going to give her the story.'

'There's probably not going to be much to tempt her in a World War Two history, surely?' said Kate.

'Not the military stuff, sure,' I said. 'But who knows what the letters will turn up? The human interest angle – that's what she's after.'

'Letters: that reminds me. An interesting-looking one arrived for you today. I've put it on your desk,' said Kate.

I nodded, and we moved on to local news – someone we all knew was apparently being a complete bastard to his wife, and though Amelia had apparently recounted the tale to Kate before I arrived the details had to be exhumed and raked over again for my benefit. I had some doubts about the veracity of all this given the known penchant for exaggeration by the lady concerned, but I was outnumbered, and wasn't much of a fan of her husband anyway.

I contented myself with sympathetic noises until I could beat a tactful retreat to my study, taking the zip folder containing Georgina's letters with me. I put them on the table with everything else I'd acquired to date, together with the Sweetman photo, and turned to my desk.

The blue envelope of the newly arrived letter was handwritten, and addressed to 'Captain Dominic Mallory PRH'. I'd never used my military rank since leaving the Army, let alone the initials designating my former Regiment, which would have been meaningless to 95% of the population. Thus it was from someone who had a military background, and almost certainly a regimental one.

I opened the envelope, which was postmarked Waltham-on-the-Wolds, the opposite end of Leicestershire from us – about thirty miles away.

Dear Dominic (if I may),

I have been informed of your wish to speak to individuals who served in Prince Rupert's Horse during the European campaign of 1944–45.

I was a nineteen year old tank Troop Leader when the Regiment landed in Normandy – one of the very few employed in that role to come through unscathed. I did not keep anything by way of an organised diary, but I do have some recollections and observations from that time which may interest you. I regard that period as the high point of my life.

If you would like to meet for this purpose please do call to arrange a time.

Yours sincerely

Simon Stonton

***

So I was right. I put the letter down for a moment and thought.

Leicestershire is really quite a small place, and veterans of Prince Rupert's Horse were not a large community within it. I had long been on the Leicestershire & Rutland regional committee of the Army Benevolent Fund, and fancied that I could recall Simon Stonton as a frequent presence at our fundraising events – always in a Rupert's tie. He had thinning red hair, I recalled. We'd exchanged a few pleasantries given our shared regimental heritage, albeit from different eras, but had never had a substantive conversation.

There and then I decided to call him the next day.

I emerged from my study slightly dreading that Amelia would still be hanging about, but she'd clearly caught the atmospherics and headed home. Kate didn't seem unduly put out.

'Who was the letter from?' she asked.

'An old boy who lives over in Waltham – he served in the Regiment at the right time. I've met him a couple of times I think. He's offered to have a chat with me. I'll fix it up tomorrow.'

Kate nodded, gave me a smile and began bustling around the kitchen. I knew when I was being dismissed – *The Archers* was on.

CHAPTER SEVEN

Because of what happened later I've been outlining a rough sequence of inter-linked events which were peripheral to my main project, but this shouldn't detract from the fact that overall it was coming together nicely.

Despite the passage of so many years since the war I soon had a gratifyingly promising group of interviewees lined up, Simon Stonton included, although I hadn't yet embarked upon the process of actually talking to them. A lot of good photographs had emerged from my various trawls, many of which had never been published before – I just had to get them into context, and check the understandably rather opaque commentaries which families (sometimes two generations younger) had provided with them.

However, niggling at the back of my mind still was the apparently recalcitrant padre, Nick Carson, whom I had not yet tried to contact. To be honest I'd been ducking it, and gathering the low hanging fruit. However, having carried over that particular item once too often in my weekly to-do lists, the day came when I finally decided to grasp the nettle. He was old: it would be foolish to miss the chance to talk to him.

It wasn't difficult to get a number given that I had his address. I thought I'd call rather than waste days on a letter which might never be answered. I dislike cold calling, but needs must.

There was no initial response, and nor did the phone kick through to an answering machine: I was on the point of giving up, vaguely relieved, when suddenly the call was picked up.

'Hello?'

The voice was clearly that of an old man, but it also sounded alert. I launched clumsily into my prepared spiel.

'Er – good morning. Am I speaking to Mr Nicholas Carson? Or Reverend Carson, if you prefer?'

'You are,' came the reply, cautiously. 'I seldom use my clerical title these days.'

'Oh – well, Mr Carson,' I continued. 'My name is Dominic Mallory—'

'What do you want?' said the voice, surprisingly sharply.

'I am a former officer in Prince Rupert's Horse,' I replied defensively. 'I am writing a new history of the Regiment in World War Two, with specific focus on D-Day and beyond.'

There was no reply, though I could hear laboured breathing.

'I wondered if you might be prepared to talk to me about those days?' I continued, and gritted my teeth: moment of truth.

His reply was a long time coming, to the extent that I was about to speak again, though I was well aware from plentiful interviews of aspiring employees that hasty qualification during sustained silence is seldom advantageous.

Finally there was something like a sigh. 'Perhaps it's time.'

***

A couple of days later I came back in the evening from a board meeting somewhere to find Kate sitting at the table in my study. I'd told her about the Carson conundrum, and the meeting I'd arranged with him in a fortnight's time: she was becoming increasingly fixated on the whole saga.

My wife was hovering again over some of the letters I'd uncovered, and as she rose to give me a kiss she looked pleased with herself. I knew better than to rush her, and waited to find out why.

We were on our second drink before she got round to the point, as I knew she eventually would.

'I've discovered something,' she said coyly. 'I think you'll be pleased.'

'Clever you,' I responded noncommittally. 'What?'

'You remember those letters your Georgina produced?'

This recent phrase was becoming rather galling, but I didn't want to show that. 'Sure.'

In truth I'd found Georgina's letters pretty disappointing. The ones in Michael Sweetman's possession, from his supposed wife, were bland and almost childlike: of course she would have been in her very early twenties. Those he had sent to his sister – Georgina's mother – were intended to conceal the reality of war rather than to show it. I saw little use for them.

Kate picked up one of the letters casually, and I awaited the big revelation. She'd studied law, but never practised, and this seemed one of the occasional moments she harked back to that. She handed it over to me.

'This is from the wife, right?' she said, coming to sit on the arm of my chair.

I took a sip from my drink and looked briefly at the letter. 'It is. Not very informative, is it?'

Kate smiled, and disentangled herself from the arm I'd slipped around her waist. She made her way unhurriedly back to the table, and thence to Jazzer's boxes. She took an envelope from one of them which she appeared to select at random, but I knew her better than that. In the same languid manner she returned to her perch on my chair, and handed over this second letter.

'And this is from the woman who wrote to Jazzer's father in the desert?'

I looked at it briefly. 'Yes. So what?'

She gently took the drink out of my other hand, into which she put the first letter.

'Look at them together.' Her smile was quietly triumphant.

There was no doubt at all, and I sat there dumbfounded, looking from one letter to the other.

They were in the same hand.

***

'Well, what can that possibly mean?' I exploded.

Kate smiled, took both the letters gently away from me and sat down in the only other chair in my study, less than three feet away. We were angled at ninety degrees to each other.

'Exactly what I've been pondering ever since I discovered this amazing coincidence a couple of hours ago,' she said, settling back. 'I love a good mystery.'

'And what has your pondering led you to conclude?'

'Well,' she said contentedly. 'Consider: one – Rowena was

writing to both men: Giles in the desert and then Michael in France. Two – she was apparently married to Michael sometime before France. Three – she married Giles five years after the war.'

'And four,' I said, 'she's Jazzer's mother.'

'Plus – five; she's still alive,' Kate added. 'Surely you've got to interview her?'

I paused to reflect. That might be difficult.

'Well, it would certainly explain why Giles received no letters from Rowena in France, as you pointed out the other day,' I said after a while. 'Looks like she ran off with someone else.'

'Must have been awkward within the same Regiment,' reflected Kate, and then looked up with her big grey eyes. 'I'm a good detective, aren't I?'

I could see that she was waiting on my approval, so I leaned forward and gave her a little kiss.

'You are,' I said. 'Genuinely. Thank you.'

And I meant it; I would never have noticed such a thing, and was grateful. Kate retreated happily to the kitchen and *The Archers*, whilst I sat back with my depleted whisky to reflect upon her unexpected discovery.

It didn't take me long to make a decision on it. Two, in fact.

***

In terms of my forthcoming regimental history, it was very probably meaningless. But as regards human interest, there was almost certainly a story there.

I knew exactly who might be intrigued by that, especially as it seemed to involve her uncle.

Whatever this story might be, it wasn't mature enough yet to push it Georgina's way, so I set it aside for the time being until I could do a little further digging to establish whether it had legs.

It was definitely intriguing though, and I decided as a result to do some detailed background research into the period between the Regiment's return to England from North Africa and its subsequent deployment to France. The apparent transfer of Rowena's affections had happened then, and it would also be a useful exercise in establishing the personal dynamics between assorted regimental characters, which might prove illuminating when it came to writing about them in action together.

So I set about revising the period I intended to ask my various interviewees about to include rather more prominently this pre-invasion period.

In tandem I thought a little gentle reconnaissance regarding Kate's discovery might prove worthwhile. Accordingly, when I was a bit stumped for anything else to do a couple of days later and didn't want to actually write anything (heaven forbid!) I called Charlie Manning.

'Dom,' he said on picking up, obviously having recognised my number. 'How goes the great endeavour?'

'Well enough,' I replied, 'though I could do with a little advice.'

'Of course,' Charlie replied, portentously. I could sense him preening. 'Fire away.'

'Odd question,' I said. 'Can you fill me in on Rowena?'

I sensed Charlie's surprise. 'As in Montagnon? Jazzer's mother?'

'Yes. I know she wrote to Giles in the desert. I just

wondered whether you thought she might be up for an interview. She was obviously closely involved with the Regiment on the eve of D-Day. I thought she might have an interesting perspective. I mean, what sort of shape is she in?'

'Well,' said Charlie, somewhat doubtfully. 'She's in fairly good nick I think. I could ask Jazzer, I suppose.'

You'll notice that I hadn't mentioned the Michael Sweetman aspect, which I thought might give Charlie a fit of the vapours at the prospect of any sort of regimental scandal – not that I wanted to deceive the poor chap, but I needed him to help rather than obfuscate. I could always plead ignorance if anything which caused embarrassment came to light.

But at that point it simply hadn't.

I thanked Charlie, and put the phone down. It wasn't more than fifteen minutes before he called back. It was a negative message, though he didn't seem at all worried at having to deliver it.

'Jazzer says no. It'll upset her.'

CHAPTER EIGHT

Kate was out that day, so I fixed myself a kitchen lunch from whatever was in the fridge, looked briefly at where Simon Stonton fitted into the regimental order of battle in Sam Lane's pre-D-Day album (2nd Troop Leader, B Squadron), reviewed my list of questions and then set out at about 2.15 pm.

I don't go to that part of North East Leicestershire very often, but it's a pleasant drive to Waltham via Melton Mowbray, and I was there in good time. I'd allowed a bit extra to find Simon's house, but it was easy enough to do, and much as I expected: rather a small cottage; Victorian I thought. He was of an age to have down-sized some years ago.

As I approached up the path Simon opened the front door, wearing a sports jacket, cords and regimental tie. He smiled weakly, and I saw his gaze slide over my shoulder to the Alfa parked in the road on the other side of the low garden wall.

'Welcome, Dominic,' he said, as we shook hands. He nodded at my car.

'Do you know, my father refused after the war ever to have any vehicle made in Germany, Italy or Japan. Stuck to it for the rest of his life. Peugeots, Renaults, Volvos and Saabs.'

I was somewhat nonplussed, and was still thinking of an answer as I crossed the threshold.

Simon turned to me as he closed the door. 'My brother was killed, you see,' he said. 'Navy. 1941.'

'I'm sorry,' I said, still on the back foot. 'How awful.'

He smiled cheerily enough at my trite response. 'Never mind. It was a long time ago. Come and meet Ann.'

He shuffled through to the front room, where his wife was waiting primly on a chair against the wall. She stood as we came in, and I could see that she had prepared tea and biscuits – a silver pot, and only two cups.

Simon introduced us: Ann said nothing, but offered a shy smile and a tiny, bird-like hand. She was probably not much more than five feet tall, and slim with it, but the remnants of petite beauty were still there. I couldn't recall ever meeting her before.

'Mrs Stonton – this is so kind of you,' I said.

She smiled again, and in a cut class accent redolent of the young Queen, to whom she must have been very similar in age, said a single word. 'Tea?'

I accepted of course, and she poured a cup for her husband too.

'Are you not joining us?' I inquired, more out of politeness than anything else.

She shook her head vigorously as if I'd made a vulgar suggestion, and Simon smiled tolerantly.

'Ann doesn't like talking about the war,' he explained. 'Of course, she lost some friends.'

I hadn't considered this, but of course there was no reason she shouldn't have done given that she looked much the same age as Simon. I knew that he'd been nineteen in 1944, so born in 1925, which made him about eighty now. Her too, then. I nodded at Simon's answer.

'I quite understand.'

With another of her reserved smiles and a nod of acknowledgment, Ann moved quietly towards the door. Simon closed it behind her, and motioned me to sit in an armchair. He sat down opposite me on the sofa and took a sip of his tea.

'So,' he said. 'Where do we begin?'

***

I set up the small tape recorder I had brought with me, opened my notepad, clicked my ballpoint pen and then looked up at my host.

'I thought we might start before 1944,' I said. 'I'd like to understand your family background, and your route into the Army. And specifically into the Regiment.'

Simon reflected briefly, and then nodded. 'Fine.'

He thought for a moment before beginning.

'My father was a solicitor. He'd served in the First World War, but only on the legal side. Nonetheless he'd spent plenty of time in France, and like everyone of that generation he saw some horrors. He knew what war was, and he had two sons, so he was very keen to avoid another major conflict. Great supporter of Chamberlain.'

'Where did you grow up?'

'Just outside Norwich, which was where my father

worked. Gresham's School. That's where most people in the county of my sort of background went. Of course, the great and the good generally went further afield – Eton or Harrow.'

'And why the Army?'

'Well, my brother was four years older than me, and was called up in 1939. My mother's father had been in the Navy throughout the first war, and had come through unscathed. He was still alive, and pushed hard for Tim to follow in his footsteps. My parents concurred. It seemed a safer option. But of course...'

'You said 1941. Where?'

'Off Crete; 22nd of May. HMS *Gloucester*, a light cruiser. Tim was a Sub-Lieutenant. Bombed and sunk. Over seven hundred dead.'

He sounded fairly phlegmatic.

'So when it came to your turn...'

'Not the Navy. I thought about the RAF, but my eyesight wasn't good enough to be a pilot, which was all I was interested in. So it was the Army, by default really.'

'And Prince Rupert's Horse?'

'Pretty much a fluke, though I volunteered for tanks. When I began training in 1943 they were still overseas of course. I became friends with someone who had regimental connections, which counted in those days, even in wartime.'

***

'Still does,' I said. 'Family Regiment.'

Simon shrugged. 'Well, he was going there, so I had an "in". I was thrilled: a crack cavalry Regiment back from the desert.'

'Who was your friend?'

The old man smiled sadly. 'John Darcy. He was killed. Not in the way you imagine – car accident. April 1944. Drink…'

'What a waste,' I said.

'It was. There was a great deal of waste in those days.'

'Tell me about the training.'

'I did six months in the ranks, at Bovington in Dorset – quite an eye-opener for a sheltered middle-class boy, I can tell you, but I was grateful for it later. That's where I met John. There were several of us hoping to be picked up for commissions. We went on to Sandhurst together for another six months.'

'Where did you join the Regiment?'

'Thetford, in East Anglia. Not far from home. They were under canvas.'

'Pretty intimidating, I imagine,' I said, remembering my own butterflies when I'd joined in peacetime as a graduate of twenty-two. To join a Regiment of such recent combat experience as a sprog officer of nineteen hardly bore thinking about.

Simon laughed ironically.

'You could say that. My Troop were all veterans of the desert, bar two. Nineteen of us all told: three Shermans each with a crew of five, and a Sherman Firefly with a bigger gun, which meant it could only fit in four. Some Regiments organised things differently, but that's how we did it. Initially they all treated me as some sort of curious pet. But I was very lucky in my Troop Sergeant.'

I smiled, remembering the splendid Sergeant Howell who had held my hand in my own early days.

'That's a blessing. I was lucky too. Not everyone was. What was his name?'

'Sergeant Sims,' he said, his eyes watering. 'Harry Sims. One of the finest men I've ever met.'

'Was he…' I began cautiously.

Simon shook his head vigorously. 'No – nothing like that. He's still alive, but in a home. Dementia. I visited him last month. He still recognised me.'

It was said with quiet emotion. I paused whilst Simon collected himself.

'Saved my life you know – more than once. He was all of twenty-four when we went to France. He had the Firefly. He took both the youngsters of course. And also the best gunner!'

We were getting ahead of ourselves.

'Tell me about some of your fellow officers when you joined. This may help.'

I passed across Sam Lane's 'Eve of D-Day' album, and Simon looked through it silently for at least a minute. I knew he'd speak when he was ready.

Eventually he cleared his throat.

'You know, this is remarkable,' he said, eyes still on the album. 'I remember us all having our pictures taken for it. But I never saw the end result. Probably too busy getting de-mobbed at the end of the war. Often wish I'd stayed in…'

He looked up at me. I dragged him back to the topic at hand.

'Why don't we start from the top?' I said gently. 'Commanding Officer.'

Simon turned back to the first page, and contemplated 'The Wolf' dispassionately.

'I was very junior,' he said, 'and of course he was a God-like figure to me. I had an interview with him when I first arrived, which may have lasted ten minutes. After that I doubt I exchanged more than a few words with him. Junior officers tended to avoid Regimental Headquarters if they could.'

I remembered the feeling. 'Well liked?'

'I think there was a certain undercurrent from those who had been in the desert, because of course he hadn't been. But mostly unspoken, at least to someone like me. He was a stickler on dress, and that didn't always go down very well: people had got used to wearing pretty much what they liked.'

'Competent?'

'I think so, at least in the administrative sense: he knew the book. But he hadn't seen action. It worried him I expect, and it certainly concerned those who had.'

'How do you know that?'

'I remember the attitude of Toby Grundy, my Squadron Leader, when he came back from a Regimental Orders Group during the first exercise I ever took part in. He was fed up, because there was virtually no time left for him to brief us, and none at all for us to brief our Troops – it was literally a case of "follow me". And I understand it wasn't the first time.'

'So poor battle procedure?'

Simon looked up with a faint smile. 'I'm not sure we called it that then. But ultimately, yes. I'm sure the orders delivered at RHQ were immaculate in terms of Staff College theory, but you've got to leave time for subordinates to pass them on and refine them. And he seldom did.'

It was a common enough phenomenon, even in my time. My own Squadron Leader in the 1980s, who had Dhofar combat experience, opined strongly that the format for delivering formal orders was for the guidance of the wise and the obedience of fools. It didn't seem that 'The Wolf' took such an expedient approach.

'Frustrating. Didn't the other RHQ officers do anything about it?'

'I'm sure they tried. You'd have to ask them.'

I wasn't aware that any of them were still alive, but let it pass.

'It must have been a shock when he was killed.'

Simon shook his head. 'Not really. I don't think I even heard about it for a day or two. I was too busy trying not to get killed myself.'

***

We worked our way gently through the album, and I still have the notes of that conversation – mostly minor characters in this story. Bobby Lomax, the Second in Command – 'cheery'; Alastair Gill, the Adjutant – 'always looked worried'; Toby Grundy; B Squadron Leader – 'unflappable: I worshipped him.' I'll only cover three of them in any depth here.

The first to crop up was Giles Montagnon. Bear in mind that at this point we were talking about the pre-embarkation period, when Giles was C Squadron Leader.

'I was always pretty wary of him,' said Simon frankly. 'A great reputation in the desert, well earned, and much admired by everyone. But he wasn't my Squadron Leader, so I kept a deferential distance. Pleasant enough, but he didn't waste time on anyone not yet fully accepted by the Regiment. And at that point I hadn't been.'

'Surprised when he took command?'

'Relieved actually. I thought it might be Toby, and I wanted him to stay as B Squadron Leader.'

The next was Nick Carson, the padre.

'Tough,' said Simon, decisively. 'He looked very young, but even the lairiest Troopers knew instinctively not to take any liberties. Mind you, they wouldn't with Trooper Ryan around, who was his Man Friday, and built like a brick outhouse. Nick arrived just before me, but had already achieved a level of respect amongst all ranks which it took me over six months in action to achieve, if I ever did. A highly, highly moral man. He genuinely meant it, you could tell.'

I flipped deliberately to the A Squadron page, and asked about Michael Sweetman, telling Simon that I had received a letter from his niece.

'Ah, Michael,' said Simon, with a sad sigh. 'Different Squadron of course, so I didn't know him that well, but he was the beau ideal of a cavalry Troop Leader. Very popular, demonstrably competent, got on with almost everyone. And good looking, which he certainly made the most of. To actually get married! It made the rest of us rather envious.'

'So a paragon?' I inquired.

'Most of us certainly thought so,' concurred Simon. 'He did have his detractors though.'

'Who?' I asked.

'Giles Montagnon, for one,' said Simon reflectively. 'He never liked Michael. Of course, there was history there.'

CHAPTER NINE

We spent so long discussing personalities that there was little time to talk about what actually happened once the Regiment had landed in Normandy. I apologised to Simon when we got to 5.30 pm, because Kate and I were going out to dinner that night: I had to go.

'Could I come again?' I asked. 'It's been a fascinating discussion.'

'By all means,' said Simon, amiably. 'It's amazing what one remembers when talking about it. Much better than trying to recollect alone. I've enjoyed it.'

We arranged a further meeting in ten days' time, and he showed me out. There was no sign of Ann.

When I got home it was getting dark, and I barely had time for a quick bath before Kate and I had to head out to the Frobishers. Neither of us much wanted to go: still, we had asked them a few weeks before; they were clearly repaying the hospitality, and it would have been churlish to refuse.

Beyond that, as Kate well knew I wasn't generally one to turn down an invitation. She sometimes said that I would willingly go to the opening of an envelope.

Once we were settled in the car and had gone a mile or so Kate turned the radio off: unusual.

'What?' I said, looking across at her.

'Your Georgina called this afternoon,' she said nonchalantly.

'She is not my Georgina,' I replied, trying and no doubt failing to conceal my irritation.

'She's rather nice, actually,' said my darling wife. 'We had quite a chat.'

'What on earth about?' I replied, with the first stirrings of unease, though I had nothing to reproach myself for.

'Well – that's it,' said Kate, a little guardedly. 'I've possibly been a tiny bit indiscreet.'

Though my eyes were on the road I could picture the little pout she always used with that tone.

'Go on.'

'Well, she explained that she'd given you those letters, and I told her how interesting I'd found them.'

I looked briefly across at her, and said nothing.

'I am interested in them, you know that,' she said defensively.

'OK – so...?'

'I got a bit carried away. I told her about the handwriting match.'

'Forgetting, of course, that she's an investigative journalist?' I said ironically, as calmly as I could.

I'd intended to tell Georgina this news myself in good time, and was rather looking forward to it, which was annoying enough. The revelation was also premature, which made it worse.

'Yes,' said Kate, meekly. 'I couldn't wait to tell her how clever I'd been. Silly, I know. Sorry.'

It wasn't often I held the moral high ground over Kate, but I was an experienced enough husband not to exploit that situation. I smiled across at her.

'Not to worry, darling, and thanks for telling me. No harm done, I'm sure.'

Kate touched my hand briefly on the gearstick, and turned the radio back on.

***

It wasn't a bad evening: we knew everyone there bar one couple, and as luck would have it I found myself placed next to the female half of that pairing at dinner.

Lois Laidlaw, she was called. About my age probably, buxom and handsome in that horsey sort of way which Leicestershire seems to specialise in. Over the first course we fenced verbally in the normal sort of introductory way: where do you live; what brought you to this part of the world; what do you do etc.

It turned out that Lois was a solicitor, as was her husband Ivor, whom I'd chatted to briefly before dinner. They'd both recently joined a practice in Market Harborough. Ivor was sitting next to Kate, and I could see that they were going through the same sort of exploratory ritual. He was probably a bit older than his wife – over fifty, at least.

Lois was amusing enough, but inevitably there came a lull in the conversation. I jumped in with both feet.

'It's a happy coincidence that you're a solicitor,' I said, 'because I'm writing a book: a factual one. It might upset some people. Do you have any advice?'

I meant it lightly, but Lois pursed her lips thoughtfully.

'How long ago did the events you are writing about happen?'

So inevitably the story of my embryonic regimental history came out.

'I think you'll be alright after sixty years,' she said reassuringly.

'Family aspect,' I said, and explained the Montagnon angle, without mentioning names.

'Interesting situation then,' Lois continued thereafter. 'See what you uncover. It's not my specialist sphere, but I'll happily give you an informal view at that point if you want to publish anything you're worried about.'

She saw me hesitate.

'A free view, before you ask,' she smiled.

I grinned back. 'Touché. That's very good of you.'

We got away at much the same time as everyone else; one of those 'breaking of the dam' situations where the first couple makes a move and everybody else follows swiftly on.

'Not too bad, was it?' I said to Kate, as we did up our seat belts.

'I could see you didn't think so,' she replied. 'What was that woman's name again? Louise?'

'Lois,' I corrected her. 'Very easy. She offered to help advise me on legalities if need be. Must be my blue eyes.'

I could sense Kate raising her eyes to the heavens. There was a pause. Then she responded.

'What do you mean, offered to help you?'

I explained.

'Oh, that. Well, she may have been easy enough to talk to, but her husband certainly wasn't. Hard work.'

I glanced across at her.

'Not like you to say that: you can usually jolly anyone along.'

'Completely impervious to my feminine wiles: collects stamps, and religious to boot.'

Not my wife's cup of tea at all.

'My poor darling,' I said. 'How can I cheer you up?'

Kate's hand crept onto mine once more, resting on the gearstick.

'I'm sure you'll think of a way once we get home,' she said quietly.

I had no need, because I knew that tone. No other conversation was necessary, and I didn't dawdle.

What a woman.

***

A fortnight or so passed uneventfully, and then one Friday morning in late July I got another interesting-looking letter amongst the usual dross.

The corporate envelope evoked the vague sense of dread in me that such things always do. I opened it, and stared in astonishment. It was from a firm of solicitors in Salisbury, and offered me 'substantive information relating to your recent inquiries' in exchange for signing a non-disclosure agreement.

The firm went by the name of J. A. Doody & Son, and the particular partner who had written to me on her expensive headed paper was called Jennifer Acland.

I called her direct line immediately, and she picked up straightaway. I explained who I was, and she responded warmly, sounding both friendly and pleased.

'Mr Mallory, how good to hear from you.' A middle-aged voice, oozing competence: sometimes you just know.

'Thank you. Regarding your letter, which arrived today – I was wondering if you could possibly give me an inkling of what this is about? I have no idea why anyone should want me to sign a non-disclosure agreement.'

'Well, my client has learned that you are engaged in writing a regimental history, which I presume is correct? Remind me of the regiment...'

I could hear papers rustling down the line.

'Prince Rupert's Horse. Yes, that is correct.'

'And you are seeking background information to, I quote – "bring events to life", is that not so?'

I recognised the phrase from the blurb I had asked Charlie Manning to publish on the website.

'I am indeed.'

'My client is in possession of such information.'

'May I ask the name of your client?'

The solicitor paused. 'The information is potentially sensitive. My client does not want to be revealed as the source.'

'Well, it would be difficult for me to include anything controversial without either attributing it or having documented evidence, as I'm sure you appreciate. Is it the sort of information that I might be able to confirm from other sources once I know what it is?'

There was a further hesitation. 'Possibly, but not in any detail.'

'Would your client be prepared to meet me to discuss this information?'

'I will certainly ask.'

I noticed that Ms Acland was careful in not revealing the gender of her client.

'Please tell him – or her – that if I decide not to use the information I undertake to treat anything revealed with absolute discretion. If I wish to use it I am certainly prepared to discuss the question of an NDA.'

Jennifer pointedly did not fall for my little ruse. 'I will certainly communicate that. It seems a sensible way ahead. Would you be happy to travel to Salisbury for such a meeting?'

'In principle, yes. At your offices, I presume?'

'Here, yes. I will come back to you with some suitable dates.'

We rang off after a few pleasantries, and I sat at my desk frowning. I was none the wiser.

***

Though it was a Saturday, the next morning I checked my emails in my home office whilst I was making Kate a coffee after feeding the dogs, and found that Jennifer Acland, the Salisbury solicitor, had emailed me rather late the previous evening.

In sum, she said two things: firstly that her client (gender still unrevealed) did not wish to see me face to face at this stage, and wished Jennifer to meet with me alone.

And secondly, she had to attend a family funeral in Northumberland on the following Thursday, hence she would be out of the office from Wednesday: could I possibly meet before then? She could offer any time on Monday or Tuesday that suited me.

Nowadays of course you'd probably hold such a short notice meeting on Skype, or Zoom, but video-conferencing wasn't an option for the average person back in 2005. Email aside, we were still largely in the analogue era, so I checked my desk diary. Monday was clear, so I emailed Jennifer to the effect that I could be in Salisbury by 11 am, and asked her to confirm.

Kate was still languishing in bed when I returned upstairs with her coffee.

'I'll be out on Monday,' I announced, climbing back in as she took her first sip, and displacing a spaniel which had crept upstairs after its breakfast.

'Oh?' she said, faintly surprised.

'Jennifer,' I said; deliberately mysterious. Kate played along.

'Georgina; Jennifer – honestly, I lose count,' she said.

'Yes, it can be exhausting,' I continued. 'But as you may have noticed, I'm here with you, not them.'

Kate looked across at me thoughtfully for a few seconds, took a further sip and then very deliberately placed her cup on the bedside table.

'So you are,' she said, turning back to me.

CHAPTER TEN

Nowadays you can pretty much guarantee some sort of hold up on the A34, but in those days it was a pretty easy run down to Salisbury from Leicestershire, and I diverted off via Wantage and Hungerford: I wanted to pass through Tidworth Garrison en route for old times' sake. It looked much the same, albeit rather more encumbered with fencing than I remembered when Rupert's had been based there in the early eighties: indeed I had joined the Regiment there. Post 9/11 security, I surmised, though back in the day we seemed to have managed perfectly well without such ugly eyesores at a time when there was a significant IRA threat.

I arrived in Salisbury in very good time, and had a restorative coffee after parking my car and establishing where Doody's offices were. They looked reassuringly old fashioned.

So did Jennifer Acland when I met her. She was in her mid-fifties, dressed in a prim business suit; without much make-up, and she had not tried to prevent her hair from greying: I had her down as a spinster till I noticed the generously sized ring on her finger. I accepted another cup of coffee, at some risk to my bladder, and sat back to hear what she had to say.

She pursed her fingers before she spoke, and paused for a moment, though I had little doubt she had already thought through how she would approach the meeting.

'It is unfortunate that my client does not wish to see you at this point,' she said, 'because I have no doubt that he – or she – is in a much better position to explain the nature of the information we are here to discuss than I am. But I will do my best.'

I nodded, took one of the biscuits she had thoughtfully provided and waited for her to continue.

She paused again. 'My client is adopted.'

'I understand,' I said, by way of encouragement. She shook her head.

'I don't think you do,' she said. 'The birth mother has no idea that my client has tracked her down. Nor that he has conducted considerable research into the family history.'

I noted the slip. 'May I ask who the birth mother is?' I enquired tentatively.

'She is now Mrs Rowena Montagnon,' said the solicitor calmly.

I was stunned. Jazzer's mother. I thought quickly.

'Can you reveal the date of that adoption?'

She answered without hesitation.

'It was finalised on the thirteenth of April 1945.'

Well before Rowena had married Giles. My brain was grinding through the implications.

'So – is that the information? I cannot see that it has any bearing on regimental history.'

Jennifer sighed.

'It is somewhat more complex than that. My client avers that his father was deliberately killed whilst on active service with Prince Rupert's Horse in Northern Europe.'

'Do you mean murdered?' I replied, astonished.

'That is the word my client used, yes,' replied the lawyer, coolly. 'He is an emotive gentleman. I do not think such a charge would stand up in court.'

'But—'

'More like deliberate exposure to harm.'

'And your client's supposed father is…' I began.

I already knew the answer.

'Michael Sweetman.'

***

Our discussion thereafter was long and wide ranging, and strayed some way from the matter at hand, because we liked each other. But eventually we returned to the point.

'So, what you are saying is that if I agree to sign this NDA your client will provide corroboration of this allegation about his father, but I am prevented from declaring the source,' I said.

'That is so.'

I reflected for a moment. 'I am sure you can see my problem. I am writing a military history, not a scandal sheet. How can he prove this assertion? And even if I decided to use it, which I am not minded to, if I am prevented from declaring my source then clearly I am setting myself up for a fall with anybody who values the Regiment's reputation. As indeed I do myself.'

The lawyer was almost meek in her response. 'I understand.'

'How does he know this, anyway?' I continued.

Jennifer was quick to respond. 'I am afraid I cannot reveal that. My client will do so himself provided you sign the NDA.'

'Well – on balance, I think not. I'm sure you understand.'

'I do indeed,' replied Jennifer. 'I will convey your decision to my client.'

***

On the drive home I kept the radio off, and mulled through the ramifications of what I had heard.

I was quite certain I had been right not to sign the NDA, as I had no wish to use the material – it was surely irrelevant to the story of the Regiment's service in Europe after D-Day. But of course it was still highly intriguing to me on a personal level.

After pausing for a sandwich at Cherwell services as I headed back north, I arrived home just after 3 pm. Kate greeted me with a peck on the cheek as I entered the kitchen, with the dogs milling cheerfully around.

'Useful?' she asked.

'Not so much useful as interesting,' I replied. 'Let's have a cuppa and I'll tell you all about it.'

Kate bustled around, and a couple of minutes later we were sitting opposite each other across the island.

'So – go on,' she said.

'Right – and you are probably not going to believe this – Rowena Montagnon gave up a child for adoption in April 1945.'

Kate's eyes widened. 'What? So that means—'

'She not only married Michael Sweetman: she had a child with him.'

'And she married Giles in—'

'1950,' I interrupted. 'Having apparently wiped the slate clean by giving up Sweetman's child for adoption.'

'Phew.'

'And furthermore, she doesn't know that the chap who was adopted – her son it seems – has tracked her down. He's the one who wants me to sign the NDA.'

'I don't quite understand…' began Kate, cautiously.

'Because there's more to it than that,' I replied. 'He's asserting that his father was deliberately put in harm's way whilst serving with the Regiment, which led to his death. He actually used the word "murder" apparently, though his solicitor doesn't think that's merited.'

'Who does he hold responsible?'

I shook my head. 'We didn't get that far: I wouldn't sign the NDA, because the allegation is not pertinent to the history of the Regiment. But I thought about it on the way home. I think it's pretty clear.'

'Who?'

'Well,' I began. 'We know Rowena wrote to Giles in the desert. Then she apparently wrote to Michael in France. Now it seems she married and had a child with him. The dates fit. Let's assume the child was conceived in May 1944, just before the invasion. It would be born in February 1945. Adoption finalised a couple of months later, after Michael's death.'

Kate leapt up, and vanished into my office, off the kitchen. She returned a few seconds later, brandishing the letters, and placed two of them in front of me: one written to Giles and the other to Michael. Then she moved behind me, placing her arm around my shoulder as I perched on my stool.

We looked first at the ones Michael had received. His wife had used a pet name ('Bunny'), so the signature wasn't conclusive, but then we checked the letters to Giles again. Those were definitely signed 'Rowena'.

'Tell me I'm not going mad,' she said. 'There's no doubt it's the same person writing, is there?'

'No,' I confirmed. I didn't even need to look at them. 'No doubt at all.'

'And three days after D-Day,' I continued, 'Giles was commanding the Regiment in which Michael was a junior officer. Circumstantially, it stacks up, doesn't it?'

'It absolutely does.'

***

As soon as I decently could the next morning I gave my new friend Lois Laidlaw a ring (the business card she'd given me at the Frobishers included her mobile), and asked if she could spare me five minutes. She accepted graciously, but stressed that she had an appointment in fifteen minutes time.

I explained the situation.

'You are quite right not to sign anything at this point,' said Lois.

'I think they want to let me assess the information, and then only ask me to sign if I wish to use it. Which will be difficult, because if I do, I won't be able to cite my source.'

'I would say that individual has received very poor legal advice,' said Lois. 'Seriously. They'd be taking a lot on trust.'

'Quite right too,' I protested. 'I'm an officer and a gentleman. Or was.'

Lois replied cynically, but with a hint of humour.

'"Was" being the operative word,' she said.

There was another brief pause.

'You need to find out more,' she said. 'I can't really advise you on what you know to date. But I will if you can do that. Got to go.'

She was right: there was still plenty to bottom out. It would certainly help to know the birth date of the mysterious adoptee, and I would try to ascertain that if I could in tandem with the wider research I was conducting.

Likewise, I would look closely if I could into the details of Michael Sweetman's death. I consulted Billy Mullins's history, which was predictably uninformative beyond the bare details:

The Regiment suffered some officer casualties in the immediate aftermath of the operations to cross the Rhine; Lieutenant Michael Sweetman being killed by artillery fire in the bridgehead on 24 March, and Second Lieutenant Miles Gillespie being wounded and evacuated the following day in similar circumstances. Five Other Ranks were additionally killed, including Squadron Sergeant Major Ryman of A Squadron, with eleven being wounded. It was a tough twenty four hours.

However I knew I didn't have long to wait: my second meeting with Simon Stonton was due in a few days, and I wondered also if the mysterious padre might have anything to add.

Maybe Georgina Hart might know more about her uncle's death as well, I mused.

CHAPTER ELEVEN

'd enjoyed my previous meeting with Simon Stonton, and I think likewise in his case. He'd certainly done a great deal of thinking – and research – in the days since we last met. He ushered me into his cottage with a broad smile. There was no sign of Ann.

'So,' I said, once I had settled myself, and set up my recorder. 'Let's talk about the invasion now, and what it was like to be a Troop Leader. We can cover personalities as they arise if we need to.'

Simon nodded briefly in assent.

'Firstly – when did you first know it was coming?'

'We were moved down from Thetford in mid-May, to a wired camp near Petersfield, not far north of Portsmouth. We came by rail; crews on the flats with the tanks. Health and safety wouldn't like it nowadays. And then we drove the last fifteen miles: it was all splendidly organised; brilliant staff work. You cannot imagine what the south of England was like then: it was a complete armed camp.'

'Americans?'

He shook his head. 'No. They were further west; Wiltshire and Dorset. Plenty of Canadians though.'

'So it was obvious it was imminent?'

'Absolutely obvious. We weren't going to do an opposed landing – we were told we would land on D +2. But down to my level we were all issued with maps of the coastline, with names excised. Gold Beach. I forget the name of the sector.'

We spoke for over an hour before Simon even reached France: the briefings; embarkation in the specialised 'Landing Craft Tanks'; final orders; seasickness; the massive naval presence in the channel hurling shells inland; the panoply of air cover. I had to change the cassette in my tape recorder, which was twenty years old – I had bought it tax-free during my time abroad with the Army.

'Even then, I knew I was part of history,' said Simon, 'and that we would win eventually. But I also knew it would be a hell of a hard grind till we reached that point. Nobody really thinks the worst will happen to him, but I wasn't entirely sure I would survive. Troop leading is a bloody dangerous job. I'd written my last letter.'

'To…?'

'Oh, my parents of course. I was nineteen years old – a virgin. Most of us were, with a few exceptions.'

'Michael Sweetman?'

Simon grinned. 'Well of course he was married.'

'Who to?' I said innocently, though of course I knew this.

'Rowena. Lovely girl. All the officers in the Regiment were asked to the wedding, because that's what you do, but of course there had to be people left behind on duty. I was one of the most junior, so—'

'When was this?' It came out rather more pointedly than I intended, and Simon looked up curiously.

'Since you are so interested – it must have been in early May. Just before we left Norfolk, because I remember being left behind there.'

***

Fascinating as it was, the Rowena/Giles/Michael dynamic was not what I was there for, and we moved on to discuss what it was like to be a Troop Leader commanding four tanks in 1944.

'Tell me about landing in France,' I said.

Simon shrugged.

'Relatively straightforward for us. Remember this was D+2: there was still a lot of debris on the shoreline of course, and the first people in had clearly had a pretty bloody time, but everything was beginning to get organised by then. We were not under fire, and B Squadron landed exactly where we expected to on time; straight off the LCTs. There was a taped lane through what were obviously uncleared sand dunes, which caused a bit of a traffic jam, but otherwise we just pressed on to our planned rally point a couple of miles inland. It was only when I took my headphones off there that I first heard gunfire. Most of it seemed to be our own artillery firing south, but there was a bit of incoming stuff too. Not much of it was near us. Jerry didn't have to be too precise – the whole beachhead was nowhere more than four miles deep then, and anything he lobbed into it had a pretty good chance of hitting something.'

'Were you scared?'

'No; not then – more like apprehensive. It felt like waiting to go in against a fast bowler at cricket. And I was also worried about being up to it. I had men's lives in my hands, and that's a big responsibility when you're nineteen.'

'It's a big responsibility at any age. When did you first go into action?'

'That afternoon.'

'Tell me about that.'

'B Squadron were put straight in to support the 6th Leicesters, an infantry battalion, as we had done several times in training. They'd come ashore on D-Day, and had managed to take a ridge in a night attack – a bloody good effort. But they were struggling to hold onto it as they were too busy beating off counter attacks to dig in. We were pushed through them onto the forward slope to give them time and space.'

'That must have been unpleasant.'

'Well, it certainly wasn't something we'd been trained to do. The ground was pretty open, so at least the Jerry infantry couldn't sneak up on us too easily. But their artillery spotters could see us. It wasn't at all comfortable. The infantry put some standing patrols out in front at last light, and then we withdrew to leaguer. Which is what we did almost every night for the rest of the Normandy campaign.'

'And of course you were tired all the time,' I said. I remembered this from my own service, even on training exercises, which might last three weeks or so.

Simon smiled ruefully. 'It was summer, so we were lucky to be back in leaguer by about 10 pm. Then you've got to replenish the tanks with fuel and ammunition, perform maintenance, get some sort of meal together, and make sure the radio frequencies and code settings are changed after midnight. There would probably be Squadron orders for us Troop Leaders too, which I then had to refine and pass on to my individual tank commanders.'

'And up again at first light, of course?'

'More like on the move at first light. Three hours' sleep if you were very lucky, assuming you had infantry in front and didn't have to put a guard out – less otherwise. Of course our own artillery were firing all the time, and Jerry got more and more adept at mortaring likely leaguer areas, so you often had to dig a scrape, or sleep under the tank, which was risky enough in itself. It was hardly peaceful; nonetheless we all went out like a light.'

'You must have been exhausted.'

'We were. As you say, all the time. But you got used to it.'

'Did you notice a big difference once the Commanding Officer was killed?'

Simon paused. 'Not really. Remember it was only the third day, and I hadn't seen The Wolf once in that time.'

I could see he was thinking.

'But Giles Montagnon did come round very early on, I remember. Spoke to our whole Squadron, and no doubt the others too: he was good at that, which the Wolf never had been. Toby Grundy was probably pleased to have an experienced soldier commanding; someone who was also a friend. That feeling probably filtered down to us, now I think about it.'

'Tell me about the padre.'

It wasn't long till my meeting with the elusive Reverend Carson, so though I hadn't necessarily intended to bring him up my subconscious obviously decided otherwise.

Simon puffed out his cheeks. 'Magnificent man: what else can I say.'

'In what way?'

'Always up at the sharp end; didn't skulk in the rear like some others I heard about. But that wasn't the half of it.'

I waited for him to continue whilst he gathered his thoughts.

'When a tank's hit and it's penetrated, or catches fire, then it's a bloody mess, as you know. If people were wounded, they either got out under their own steam or were helped out by other crews, if that was possible. But obviously those who were dead needed to be got out afterwards, if the tank was accessible. To salvage the tanks, but above all to bury our own. Believe me, that's not a good sight for other tank crews, though inevitably sometimes we had to do it. Just body parts in some cases, or incinerated. Whenever he could, our padre did that job, to spare us having to – him and his driver, Trooper Ryan. We were bloody proud of him. So respected. And so young.'

'Fine man.'

'He was that. And in a roundabout way, he probably saved my life.'

***

We were getting side-tracked, but it was a diversion I was intrigued to follow.

'In what way?' I asked.

Simon spread his hands expressively. 'It took until August till the Normandy campaign was won, and it was a bloody hard grind against a determined defence. God knows how the Germans managed it given our complete air superiority, but they did, until the Americans broke out in the west and looped round behind those forces facing us and the Canadians, which included the bulk of Jerry armour. You'll have heard of the Falaise pocket?'

I nodded. Surrounded on three sides, the Germans had been massacred by Allied airpower as they desperately tried to escape to the east.

'Well, then there was a mad chase across France, followed by the debacle of the Arnhem operation in Holland. Everything slowed down after that: we'd outrun our supplies; we hit bad weather in the autumn, and we came up against strong German defences in the border area. The Siegfried line. The point is, by that time there were damn few of the original Troop Leaders left. In my Squadron, I was the only one. Jimmy Langstaffe was killed when his tank was mined within a week of landing. Harry Noonan was mortared and wounded in July – not too bad; lucky fellow. Charles Hope-Richards came up against a Panther tank at point blank range in November, and that was the end of him. There were a couple of replacement Troop Leaders who had come and gone in days as well. So by January 1945 I was well aware that it was probably just a matter of time. It was much the same in the other Squadrons.'

I waited for him to get round to Nick Carson's role, and Simon paused briefly before continuing.

'I wasn't scared out of my wits or anything – just a bit bomb happy I think, and resigned to the inevitable. And over-confident: started taking silly risks. I'd seen that in others, and it only ever ended one way, but I didn't recognise it in myself. Odd.'

'And?'

'Well – you've got to understand that Toby Grundy was promoted to regimental command elsewhere in October, and deservedly so. He always kept a close eye on his young Troop Leaders: he had a replacement one posted out for not being up to the job shortly before he went, and most of us had brief periods of attachment to the supply echelon when he could manage it, to reduce the strain on us. Toby's replacement came across from another Regiment on promotion to Major: chap called Adrian Morby. Quite young – he can't have been more than twenty-seven or so. He took some time to find his feet, and was simply not as adept at keeping tabs on how people were faring as Toby had been. Plus I was by then pretty experienced, so he didn't want to lose me. He leant on people where he could, which was fair enough.'

'So what did the padre do?'

'I remember having a chat with him in early January, when we were in leaguer before some blasted operation having just come out of cosy billets in a town – he was good at getting around, as I've said. It was sodding cold; we were knee-deep in snow; a friend of mine in A Squadron had recently been killed in some bloody silly accident, and I must have been pretty morose. Anyway, two days later I found myself recalled from B Squadron to Regimental Headquarters, issued with a scout car and given a role as liaison officer to the people either side of us. Not exactly a cakewalk, but a hell of a lot less risky than being a Troop Leader. At the time I thought I must have put up some sort of black, until Giles Montagnon took the trouble to interview me personally. He told me that he had recommended me for a Mention in Despatches.'

Simon was very modest about this considerable accolade,

but I could sense his quiet underlying pride. I knew already that the recommendation had been accepted: I had noticed the distinctive oak-leaf cluster on his campaign medals one Remembrance Sunday.

'So what brought that change about?' I asked.

'Well, I know now, but I didn't then,' replied Simon. 'Although he respected individual confidences, where he could Padre Nick acted as a very shrewd pair of eyes for the Commanding Officer. He lived at Regimental HQ, and I know from Bobby Lomax that he and Colonel Giles often spent time in discussion. Command is a lonely job. I've no doubt that Giles found it useful to talk frankly to someone outside the normal regimental chain of command. And I'm equally in no doubt that in one of those talks, Padre Nick mentioned that he thought young Stonton was getting near the end of his tether.'

'And so you were moved from a front line role,' I said. It was a statement of fact.

'I was, for a month or so,' replied Simon. 'So were other people, from time to time: it was good man management by Colonel Giles.'

'But Padre Nick brought it about?' I said. The nod of assent followed quickly.

'And that is why, indirectly, I credit him for saving my life.'

***

'It must have been around then that Michael Sweetman was killed?' I asked.

I could see Simon pondering. After a while he responded.

'Later, I think. During the Rhine crossings. End of March? Easy enough to check.'

He paused to reflect again, and I waited for him to continue.

'Odd that he never got a break like me; he'd been Troop Leading ever since Normandy too; even got selected to take over Recce Troop, which is a tough job. Maybe he wasn't so obviously showing the strain.'

'Or perhaps he just wasn't fortunate enough to have had such a revealing chat with Nick Carson, which got back to the Commanding Officer,' I ventured.

Simon considered this.

'Yes. That was probably it.'

CHAPTER TWELVE

W hen I got home after a long day of interviewing I sat down to tell Kate all about it over a cup of tea.

Unsurprisingly she wasn't greatly interested in the minutiae of life and death in a tank Regiment in 1944/45, which had formed the bulk of my discussion with Simon, but did perk up at the mention of Michael Sweetman, in whom she had developed a proprietary interest since uncovering the handwriting saga.

'Well, it's obvious, isn't it?' she exclaimed. 'Giles got dumped, so he decided that Rowena's new man wasn't going to survive. And he was in a position to ensure that. Revenge.'

I considered this.

'Could be,' I said. 'But it wouldn't have been easy. Firstly, people presumably knew about the Rowena issue, so would have been alert to anything too obvious. And secondly, it's pretty damn difficult to line anybody up to be killed on somewhere as unpredictable as a battlefield. I think that's too simplistic.'

Kate was not pleased. She paused for a moment, and then headed out towards the drawing room with an ominously determined air. I waited resignedly for her return, and she was gone for some minutes. When she came back she was smiling triumphantly; a look I knew well. I braced myself for the great revelation, and a large blue book thumped down in front of me, open at particular page.

'There,' she said. 'Read that.'

I turned the book over curiously, and then looked up at her in astonishment.

'The Bible?' I inquired. 'I didn't even know we had one in the house.'

Christmas, Easter and Harvest Festival were about our churchgoing lot, with weddings, funerals and christenings thrown in whenever.

'Read,' said Kate insistently, indicating the passage with her finger. So I did.

It was quite a long section, from the Book of Samuel, and I was surprised that Kate even knew of it: the story of Uriah the Hittite, David's lust for his wife Bathsheba, and the steps he had taken to slake it. The key section read:

'And he wrote in the letter, saying: "Set ye Uriah in the forefront of the hottest battle, and retire ye from him, that he may be smitten, and die."'

I read the whole saga for the first time in about forty years, sighed, and put down the Bible.

'Nothing new, is it?' Kate asked. 'As old as history, in fact.'

'No – because there's nothing new under the sun,' I said. 'But I'm impressed you remembered the story.'

'But you still don't think that's what happened?'

'I'll keep an open mind,' I said cautiously. 'There may be

something in it. I'll explore the idea with the padre when I see him tomorrow.'

I did indeed have another long day ahead of me, and Kate knew that, so she didn't press the point.

However, I knew her well enough to know that she'd probe me rigorously afterwards.

***

It was about an hour and a quarter's drive down to Nick Carson's village just outside of Oxford, so I set off the next day for our 3 pm appointment straight after a fairly early lunch, allowing a bit of leeway for hold ups.

I was rather ambivalent about our meeting given his brusque manner on the phone, but also thought I had a fair idea of why he might have fallen out with Rupert's. Or more specifically, with its then Commanding Officer. My main focus would be more generally on his experience of the campaign from the perspective of a padre, but I intended to probe that thorny aspect too if I could.

I'd also done my background, as we authors say, and reflected on this as I drove.

Nick Carson featured in *Who's Who*, and had always been an activist priest: he'd never made Bishop – probably too troublesome – but had sat on many governmental committees and quangos; thereby going to the Lords as a Labour peer in 1972. He'd departed public life not long after the election of Margaret Thatcher in 1979, which was probably no coincidence, and thereafter had busied himself with charitable works, particularly in South Africa, where he was a voluble supporter of Nelson Mandela. He didn't appear to have been a practising clergyman since entering the political arena, and apart from the occasional article, usually in the *Guardian* or the *New Statesman*, he was effectively now retired. He had never married.

I had a fair idea from this research of the sort of person he would be, and braced myself accordingly for a whiff of sanctimony as he emerged from The Old Rectory to meet me. A rectory still actually lived in by a man of the church, I mused as I got out of my car: unusual indeed.

Nick Carson surprised me from the outset. He was a wiry figure, with snow-white hair, looking very trim for his eighty-five years, and he greeted me hospitably with an unforced grin. There was certainly something ascetic and stern about him, but he was clearly trying to be friendly. I felt guilty for pre-judging him. He reminded me of my Uncle Ralph: amiable, but with a fierce faith, the origin of which I'd never understood before his early death, because it wasn't common in our family.

As we walked inside Nick apologised immediately for his brevity on the phone when I had called.

'You caught me by surprise. I had just heard of a great friend's death. All too common I'm afraid at my age.'

The Victorian rectory was comfortable, well furnished and tidy: there was no obvious evidence of it, but I suspected the presence of a devoted housekeeper somewhere in the background. A tray was laid out in the drawing room, with a silver teapot and two cups – saucers of course; nothing so vulgar as mugs.

'So,' said my host, once he had poured, offered me sugar and handed me my cup. 'Where do you want to start?'

I finished setting up my tape recorder, and looked up

at the slim figure opposite me. His gaze was steady as he awaited my answer, and his eyes were very blue, stark against his white hair. Indubitably a man of strong character and self-confidence.

'Well, you must have been very young to be a regimental padre,' I said. 'Why don't you tell me how that came about?'

'Yes, that would be a good start point,' agreed the old man. 'You're right. I was only just ordained. I knew even before then that the people who needed me most were on the front line, not in some village parish, or even in an inner-city slum. Plus Hitler needed stopping. I volunteered.'

I nodded approvingly. '"All that is necessary for the triumph of evil is that good men do nothing." I can't remember who said that.'

'Edward Burke; supposedly. Though some say John Stuart Mill. Yes, something like that.'

'And how did you come to be with Prince Rupert's Horse?' I asked.

Nick Carson took a very deliberate sip of his tea. 'Complete fluke,' he said nonchalantly.

I waited for him to continue, as I knew he would.

'The Regiment had a much-loved and very distinguished padre called Lance Goddard, who had been with them since the outbreak of war. No doubt he was reckoned by the Royal Army Chaplains Department to be a good role model for a youngster, so they posted me to Rupert's as a sort of understudy. He was very kind to me, but I thought immediately that he seemed too old for further active service: he was approaching fifty.'

'What happened to him?'

The eighty-five year-old spread his hands expressively. 'As it happens, he really was too old. He had a mild heart attack in May, just as we were moving down south before the invasion. Nothing too serious – he lived until 1975 – but clearly he was unfit for operational deployment.'

'And no replacement could be found in time?' I asked.

'Well… not quite.' I detected a hint of embarrassment before he continued.

'The thing is – I'd been with the Regiment for over six months by then, and had settled in well. I liked them, and they liked me; so…'

'They didn't push for a replacement?'

A modest nod of assent.

'The Wolf did not push for a replacement. I think he probably also thought I would be more malleable than Lance, who was a man of decidedly firm views when it came to the men's welfare. He didn't want someone similarly robust coming in.'

'He misjudged you, then?' I smiled.

'I'm afraid he did,' replied my companion, with a sad smile. 'Of course, he never lived to realise it.'

***

We moved on to the invasion, which had left the young and almost entirely militarily inexperienced padre stunned by its scale and violence. I told him of the various people I had spoken to about those early weeks, Simon Stonton amongst them, and his face broke into a smile.

'Simon! A schoolboy! He was even younger than I was.'

'I think he grew up fast, though,' I responded.

'They all did, those young Troop Leaders – if they lived long enough. Too many didn't,' replied the priest, grimly.

After a brief discussion about the death of the Wolf, which Nick had not witnessed (though he thought 'Giles Montagnon was undoubtedly the right man to take over'), we went on to discuss the bitter fighting before the eventual breakout in August, when the British armour had suffered so badly. I asked where Nick would position himself when there was a big operation. He paused to reflect for a moment.

'It depended,' he replied. 'I started off by basing myself at the Regimental Aid Post: that was what I'd been taught in training. But that was based on World War One methodology, when everyone in the same unit was cheek by jowl. We operated in too dispersed a fashion for that to be any good.'

'So how did you change it?'

'Well – if an operation was laid on, it was generally pretty clear who was going to bear the brunt of it, or was likely to. I would generally attach myself to that Squadron. But I didn't want to be a nuisance, or a worry. I was in my jeep: probably a hedge, or a ridge line, or a corner behind the tank of the Squadron Leader I'd attached myself too. It depended on the lie of the land. You know.'

I did. 'Yes. A tactical bound,' I said. 'And I gather when tanks got knocked out you tried to deal with that situation?'

He looked up abruptly. 'Who told you that?'

'Simon Stonton mentioned it,' I replied, concerned at his tone.

He shook his head.

'Well, it wasn't always like that – it evolved. I was appalled in the early days when some of our soldiers were expected to remove people from knocked-out tanks. So I helped with one, when I could see the individuals trying to do that were distressed. It was ghastly. After that I tried whenever I could to spare them that, together with my splendid driver, Trooper Tom Ryan.'

'Tell me about Trooper Ryan. Simon Stonton mentioned him.'

The old priest looked at me askance over the rims of his glasses for an unnaturally long time. I recognised that was sizing me up.

'Did he, indeed?'

I paused, waiting for him to continue. Nick Carson sighed.

'Tom was like a great big bloodhound. Not blessed with intellect in the traditional sense, but immensely loyal. I'd helped his mother out with a housing difficulty shortly after my arrival. Thereafter he wanted very much to be my driver, to show his gratitude. Not many people fancied driving the padre around, so he got the job. He was good at it too: driving; maintaining the jeep; cooking; being on time. I was lucky to have him. He was a fine man, and became a friend.'

'And he helped you with the knocked-out tanks?'

'Well – we couldn't do it of course unless the tank was in territory held by us, nor did we always have to – there was a dedicated salvage organisation, but inevitably it got over-stretched. So I helped when I could, and Tom helped me. It wasn't often; I spent much more of my time succouring the wounded and letting people talk, if they wanted to, plus trying to make sure that nobody was left unaccounted for.'

'Nonetheless, that's the legend.'

'Legend is the word,' he said, with a 'what can I do about it?' gesture. 'I probably did it four or five times. Word gets around. People say they were there, and exaggerate.'

'You were awarded the Military Cross,' I said. 'So there was some truth in it.'

'Up to a point.'

'I understand you also spoke frequently to the Commanding Officer?'

This was the first mention of Giles other than in the context of taking over from the Wolf, and I waited keenly for his former padre to react. He was perfectly calm.

'More a case of him speaking to me, really. There were a lot of difficult choices to be made in his job, not least sacking friends who weren't up to it. He used me as a sounding board, that's true. If that helped him in any way I am glad of it.'

'And you sometimes put in a word for people?'

He looked up. 'Well, from time to time. Simon again, I take it?'

'He credits you indirectly with saving his life.'

Nick shook his head. 'I take no credit for that. But he deserved a rest: he was a brave chap who was worn out and pushing his luck.'

I hesitated for a few moments before my next question, and I saw from his wry expression that the old man had anticipated it.

'So – are you able to tell me why you resigned? And why you have maintained your distance from the Regiment ever since?'

***

'Why do you think?' he said quietly, neatly turning the tables on me.

I paused. 'Possibly it had something to do with Michael Sweetman?'

Nick's surprise was obvious, and for the first time I sensed uneasiness.

'I would be interested to learn what gave you that impression,' he said, in a deliberately neutral tone.

'Well,' I replied, 'my research indicates that Rowena had been writing to Giles whilst the Regiment was fighting in North Africa.'

I hesitated to see Nick's reaction. There was none: he simply waited, so I continued.

'And – sometime between the return of the Regiment to England and the invasion, Rowena's affections were transferred to Michael Sweetman, whom she duly married. And indeed had a child with. I've met his niece, Georgina.'

Nick's eyebrows went up slightly. 'I knew of the marriage of course; I conducted it. Not of the child, at the time,' he said.

'Some of the letters Georgina gave me were from Rowena to Michael – they came to her mother after his death. Am I near the mark in that Giles resented Michael because he'd married Rowena?' I asked.

'I cannot see why any of that would be a resignation matter for me,' he replied coolly. 'Pray explain your logic.'

There was a certain amount of steel in his voice, and I was unnerved: I was getting into the realms of conjecture, and knew it. I drew a deep breath.

'I think you were used to Giles taking your advice about people who needed a rest, as with Simon Stonton, but that he refused to do so in the case of Michael Sweetman, who had been a Troop Leader for just as long. Because he had an axe to grind with Michael Sweetman. Am I right?'

Nick sighed. 'I spoke to Giles about Simon because I

happened to have a chat with him when he was obviously down. How do you know if I had any such discussion with Michael?'

'Did you?'

'I did speak with him at one point, early in the campaign.'

'And did you mention that to Giles?'

'I did. We spoke at some length about it. As a result Michael was moved from C Squadron to become Recce Troop Leader.'

I pondered this for a moment. Recce Troop had used fast, lightly armoured Stuart tanks rather than Shermans. And it worked directly for the Commanding Officer, Giles, rather than for one of the Squadrons. It was a post for an experienced, proven Troop Leader.

'So Michael was then directly under Giles's orders, but still in a front line role, unlike Simon?'

'He was,' said Nick, quietly.

'Well, there you are,' I exclaimed. 'That's it. That's the reason you resigned. Giles was out to get Michael killed, and you knew it.'

For a moment the old padre looked nonplussed, but instantly regained his equilibrium.

'I do not recognise that circumstance at all.'

CHAPTER THIRTEEN

I got home about 7pm, and was immediately pumped for information by my eager wife. I told her the tale over a bottle of wine before supper.

'And you couldn't get any more out of him?' said Kate, disbelievingly.

I shook my head apologetically.

'Not a thing. Not on that, anyway. He said it was nothing to do with the regimental history, which was the only basis upon which he had agreed to meet me. It's a fair point.'

Kate pouted; disappointed. 'Was the rest of your talk any use?'

'Yes. I've got some good stuff on tape. He's got a memory like an elephant.'

She paused, and then returned to her principal area of interest.

'So do you think Giles did it?'

'I wouldn't rule it out. Nick Carson certainly didn't. But he wouldn't give me the whole story. To be honest, unless it's material to my history I'm not sure I greatly care. Though I admit I'm curious.'

Kate got up and poured herself a second glass.

'So am I,' she said.

***

Not much happened over the next week or so: or not much that concerns this tale, anyway.

I had a couple of meetings involving other projects in London over the course of September, and I interviewed an old boy who lived nearby in Northampton, though the material wasn't great, and I wasn't sure I could use it. In tandem with all this I started replanning the structure of my book – or in truth, planning it for the first time. I've always been of the school that believes metaphorically in just putting pen to paper and going with the flow, but this was a complex undertaking. I knew it needed more than that.

Then early in October, suddenly Georgina rang. It wasn't much past 9.30 am.

I'd put her number in my mobile, so I knew it was her, though for some odd reason I didn't admit it when I answered.

'Hello – Dom Mallory,' I said.

'Hi – it's me: Georgina. Georgina Hart,' she said, in a low voice. 'Can you talk?'

It was several weeks since we'd met, but I was oddly pleased by her conspiratorial tone. And Kate was away for the day, visiting her new-born niece.

'Sure,' I replied nonchalantly.

'I've got some news,' she said. 'It concerns your project. I wonder if we could meet?'

I certainly wasn't averse to this in principle, but she lived a fair way away.

'I'm pretty busy at the moment,' I began guardedly. Which indeed I was.

'Don't worry – I'll come to you,' she said.

'Well – when were you thinking of?' I replied.

'Today, if you can manage it. Lunch maybe? On me this time.'

I pondered briefly. A boring book planning session, or lunch with an attractive, amusing woman? I suppose someone of resolute character and iron resolve would have chosen the former, but I've never been of the hair shirt persuasion. And I'd told her I owed her a favour when we last met.

So we agreed to meet at a pub close to me at 1 pm – the Tollemache Arms at Harrington, just over the county border in Northamptonshire: it's not our local, as that would simply cause curiosity and gossip, with all sorts of people lining up to say hello whilst taking stock of my decorative companion. I did not want such a distraction; nor did I want anyone jumping to false conclusions, which would inevitably get back to Kate.

Georgina had arrived before me (I saw her car), and was sitting primly at a table in the corner when I entered the pub. I was there early myself, so that surprised me. I insisted on buying her a drink, and then we sat opposite each other looking at our menus. I glanced over the top of mine at her furrowed brow as she concentrated. She was rather a vision.

When we had both ordered and were waiting for our meals over our drinks, I looked at her expectantly.

'So – what is this news you are so keen to impart to me?' I said, light heartedly.

'I am onto something, and I thought I should let you know, as it does touch on your book,' she replied.

'Go on,' I said evenly.

'It concerns my uncle, Michael Sweetman. You remember him; the letters?' she said.

I nodded.

'He had a child. That child was adopted. I have tracked him down,' she continued.

My stomach began to flutter. 'Well, that sounds like a great human-interest story,' I began hopefully.

Georgina raised her hand briefly. 'It's a lot more than that. It's a murder story,' she said, her eyes gleaming with excitement.

'What? Don't be ridiculous,' I protested. 'What on earth do you mean?'

The waiter arrived with our food at that moment, which caused a minor delay at a critical point in our conversation, but then Georgina continued in a low voice.

'My Uncle Michael married shortly before the invasion. Rowena was previously in a relationship with Giles Montagnon – well, if not in a relationship there was at least some sort of understanding. Giles was commanding Prince Rupert's Horse when Michael was killed. The child was born shortly before his death. And that child is my source.'

She sat back to await my reaction, and I didn't like the triumphant expression on her face. Unhappily, I had a nasty feeling that what she said might well be true.

'How does he know? The child? He wasn't there,' I replied.

'He has his sources,' she said with some finality, closing off further probing.

'And are you going to publish this story?' I inquired as politely as I could.

'I am. It's what I do,' she replied. I fancied I saw a hint of nervousness.

'If you want my advice, you will not do that,' I said. 'The allegation is entirely unproven, and probably can't be one way or the other after sixty years. You will hurt people – most notably Giles's wife, Rowena, who is still alive, and his son, General Jasper Montagnon.'

'I've signed a contract,' she said defensively. 'It's the truth. I'm only letting you know this as a courtesy, because it all occurred in the time that's going to be covered by your book.'

'What's it going to appear in? And when?'

'*Daily Mirror*. Towards the end of next month.'

'Have you submitted it yet?'

'No – but I will within the next fortnight. They're going to make a big feature of it.'

It was only a year since the *Mirror* had published fake photographs allegedly showing British soldiers torturing Iraqi detainees – an episode which had cost its editor his job. I'm sure it's better now, but at the time I could not think of a publication with which the Regiment would less like to be associated, and I told Georgina so with some forcefulness, albeit sufficiently quietly not to attract attention from those eating nearby. She seemed a little taken aback at the tone of my response, but investigative journalists tend to be resilient people, and she was no exception. She stuck to her guns.

After that our meal was somewhat awkward, and our conversation stilted. We finished as soon as we decently could, I paid (Georgina's offer seemed to have lapsed – or to be charitable she probably simply forgot), and we made our way out to the car park together, where there is a splendid view across a valley. As Georgina reached her Golf she unlocked it, and turned quickly to face me.

'Well, thank you Dom,' she said.

Suddenly I could that see that she was upset; on the verge of tears.

She leaned in for an awkward kiss on the cheek, and slid nimbly into her car. Then she was gone.

***

On the short drive home I mulled over how Georgina had made contact with Rowena's supposed offspring, whom of course I had not met, having declined to sign the NDA. But I soon gave up – I had no idea; she was an investigative journalist, and they have their ways.

I also considered not telling Kate about my short-notice lunch with the woman whom she'd been rather too keen before to label as 'my' Georgina. Frankly I suspected that the root of the problem was the indiscretion my darling wife had admitted to on the way to the Frobishers, and I had no wish to rub her nose in it. But on balance, I decided I'd better come clean.

Kate was back from her sister's when I arrived home. As I suspected, once I told her she was contrite.

'This is all my fault,' she said, puckering up. Which it was, but I was too circumspect to say so. However, she could read me like a book, and the lack of a denial told her everything about what I truly thought.

'I'm off for a bath,' she declared accusingly, as if daring me to stop her.

I sighed, finished making the cup of tea she'd started

making me, and sat down to reflect. The key issue was the thorny matter of the adverse publicity Georgina's story was likely to stir up the following month, both for the Regiment in general and for Jazzer's family in particular.

I decided I had better raise a red flag. After due consideration I decided to call Charlie Manning the next morning.

After an hour or so Kate came down in her dressing gown all smiles, as I knew she would, and we made up over a drink and a TV supper. She was still chuntering about Georgina, but we were now on the same side, and later on she demonstrated very convincingly that I was forgiven.

***

I called Home HQ the next morning as planned. Sam Lane picked up, and I asked if I could speak to Charlie. There was a slight hesitation before Sam said that the Regimental Secretary was out of the office, and then an expectant pause.

'On duty?' I inquired evenly.

A hesitant cough. 'Not exactly.'

It was early October of course, the start of the pheasant season, and in an instant I realised where Charlie was.

'He's shooting, isn't he?'

Charlie was a keen shot, and a notably good one. I could tell that Sam was torn between loyalty to his superior and coming clean to someone who had clearly identified the reality of the situation. There was another cough, this time rather apologetic.

'Yes, he is Dom. Lord Walden.'

I thought quickly. 'Assuming he's back in the office

tomorrow, could you please ask him to call me, Sam? It's quite urgent.'

Sam was all calm efficiency. 'Of course. Is there anything I can do?'

I paused for a moment. Sam Lane had been in post for a long time, and I knew that Charlie trusted him implicitly. He'd also been Jazzer's RSM when the latter had been Commanding Officer of Prince Rupert's Horse, so he had skin in the game. He deserved to be told.

'You may as well know, Sam. There's going to be a piece appearing in the *Daily Mirror* either late this month or early next alleging that Colonel Jazzer's father arranged the death of a brother officer during the war whilst he was Commanding Officer. I wanted to talk to Charlie about it so that the Regiment is prepared.'

I could hear steady breathing on the other end of the line, but there was no response. 'Sam?' I said.

'That is utter balls,' came the unemotional reply eventually. 'Colonel Giles won two Distinguished Service Orders and a Military Cross. He did not have time to go around bumping off his officers.'

I told Sam the story, leaving out my strong suspicion that Kate might have been the trigger for the whole thing.

'It's all balls,' repeated Sam again at the end of my five-minute description, 'but thank you for telling us. I will let Charlie know, and I'm sure he will be in touch with Colonel Jazzer.'

As I was about to ring off he caught me with one final question.

'By the way, what's the name of this investigative journalist?'

'Georgina Hart. She's the niece of Lieutenant Michael Sweetman, whose death in 1945 is the one in question.'

There was a dismissive sniff, and I could sense Sam Lane writing the name down carefully.

'Georgina Hart. Thank you, Dom.'

***

It didn't take long for the jungle drums to start beating. My mobile rang at 9.15 am the next morning, and I recognised the Colonel of the Regiment's home number.

'Hello Jazzer,' I said resignedly, and braced myself. Except it wasn't Jazzer. It was Mary.

'He's abroad, Dom; in Canada, visiting the training area at Suffield,' she explained calmly, but I could sense her underlying anger.

'Now – would you mind repeating to me the farrago of nonsense that Charlie Manning has just attempted to explain to me. I have never heard such rubbish in my life.'

Patiently I ran through the tale once more, certain that it would have lost something in transmission from me to Sam; to Charlie and thence to the irate Lady Montagnon. She heard me out in silence.

'Who is this bloody man?' she exclaimed once I had finished.

'I don't know; I wouldn't sign the NDA. Only that he claims to be your mother-in-law's son. In other words, Jazzer's half-brother.'

'And this wretched journalist harpy does know him, does she? And she knows better than me whether I've got a brother-in-law or not?'

'Don't shoot the messenger, Mary,' I said mildly. I'd already explained that Georgina had responded to an advert I'd placed to gather material for the project Jazzer had asked me to complete.

'I'm sorry, Dom,' she said in quiet exasperation. 'I know this isn't your fault. But Rowena is eighty-three. Even assuming there's any truth in this, which I very much doubt, it's unfair to have it splashed all over the papers sixty years later. And as for the slurs on Giles's name – I'm sure we'll have to consult our lawyers. It must be defamation, or do I mean libel? Maybe we can get an injunction or something.'

I was pretty sure that the dead could not be libelled, but thought I'd let a lawyer tell Mary that.

'It's a tricky situation, I agree,' I said. 'I'm sure Jazzer will have a view on it – a pretty strong one, knowing him. When's he back?'

'The day after tomorrow,' replied Mary. 'He's going to be very cross indeed.'

CHAPTER FOURTEEN

She was right. There was a peremptory email from Jazzer two days later summoning me to a meeting with him, Charlie and Sam at Home Headquarters early the next morning. Newark is over fifty miles from me, and I had been a civilian for more than sixteen years, but clearly this cut no ice whatever with the irate General. To be fair, he'd travelled even further.

I was greeted with a mug of coffee, and we settled down around the small table in Charlie's office. The others had clearly already been in discussion (I suspect they'd deliberately met early), and I detected from their body language that it was one against three – or rather, that the other two were taking their lead from Jazzer.

'So,' began Jazzer, 'this is a pretty pickle. Dom, what have you got to say?'

He might as well have ended 'for yourself,' as if I was an errant schoolboy. I bristled.

'I have nothing to say, other than to restate the facts. Georgina Hart is the niece of Michael Sweetman, who died in March 1945 whilst serving with the Regiment. She replied to the post I put on Charlie's website asking for information once you had persuaded me to write the 1944/45 regimental history. I met her. She gave me some letters.'

Charlie shifted his seat uncomfortably. It was apparent that he had not briefed Jazzer on this aspect.

'Letters? What bloody letters?'

'Some were written by Michael Sweetman to his sister, who was Georgina Hart's mother.'

'So what?' said Jazzer aggressively.

'Others were written to him, by a woman, and were found in his personal effects after his death.'

'Again, so what?'

'That woman was your mother. Rowena.'

All three men gaped, even the undemonstrative Sam.

'How can you possibly be certain of that?' demanded Charlie.

'Because she also wrote to Colonel Jazzer's father, in the desert in 1942 and 1943,' I replied. 'Those letters were in the boxes you gave me to take away, Jazzer. Same hand. No doubt about it.'

'Go on,' said Jazzer. 'Why did you not tell me all this, Charlie?'

Charlie wilted silently under the Colonel of the Regiment's glare. In truth I hadn't explained it to Sam, so his unfortunate boss was unsighted.

Sam leant forward. 'Why shouldn't Colonel Jazzer's mother write to his father?'

I sighed as the others looked at me expectantly. 'You don't get it, do you? As Colonel Jazzer will know, his parents were married in 1950.'

Jazzer nodded, and then I saw the penny drop. His bombast deflated in an instant.

'So that's the root of it. She's going to say that my father had his apparent rival killed.'

'I think she's going to write that your father deliberately put Sweetman in harm's way, yes. Sometime during the Regiment's time in England before D-Day, it appears that Rowena's affections were transferred from one to the other.'

I didn't think it was the moment to mention the marriage, or the adoption, though it would be unusual (to put it mildly) if Jazzer had been unaware that his mother had been previously wed. But stranger things have happened.

'What can we do, Dom?' Jazzer asked. I had never seen him at such a loss.

'Not much, I think, though I suggest you confirm that by getting legal advice. I've spoken to Georgina. No dice, unless the *Mirror*'s lawyers put the kibosh on it. She's an investigative journalist, and she senses a sensational story.'

'Bloody bitch,' said Sam, quietly. 'How does she know about this, anyway?'

This was a dangerous question, and I did not want to draw attention to Kate's possible role. Accordingly I told them about the Salisbury solicitor and her mysterious client, whilst studiously omitting the adoption aspect.

'I believe Georgina Hart has tracked him down,' I said. 'He's her primary source.'

'But it can't possibly be true can it?' asked Charlie. I could see he was willing that to be the case. The thought of any scandal attaching itself to the Regiment was anathema to him.

I expected an explosion from Jazzer, but was surprised by his measured reaction.

'We must very much hope not, gentlemen. It depends upon what evidence she produces.'

There was a thoughtful silence for a moment, and after further discussion we agreed that I would approach the Salisbury solicitor again to see if she would broker a meeting for me with her client. We needed more information.

'Remind me again,' grumbled Jazzer, as we broke up, 'when is this blasted article coming out?'

'Around the end of the month, I believe,' I replied. 'We've got three weeks tops if we want to stop it.'

***

Immediately I got home I called Jennifer Acland.

After the normal introductory pleasantries I got straight to the point.

'Your client has been talking,' I said. 'Indiscreetly.'

'Indeed?' said Jennifer, in her trademark neutral style. 'Pray tell me more.'

'Well, he – and I know it is a he, by the way – has apparently been tracked down by someone called Georgina Hart. And whatever tale he has to tell, he's told it to her.'

'Who is Georgina Hart?' replied Jennifer calmly.

'That's the trouble.' I said. 'She's an investigative journalist.'

I could sense Jennifer Acland pursing her lips disapprovingly at the other end of the line. *Wait till you hear the next bit*, I thought.

'And beyond that, she is Michael Sweetman's niece.'

'Goodness gracious!' exclaimed the solicitor, which was pretty extreme coming from her.

'The issue we have – or the Regiment has, and in particular

Rowena Montagnon's son, General Jasper Montagnon – is that she has a feature article appearing in the *Daily Mirror* in about three weeks which is going to focus on your client's allegations.'

'I see.'

'General Montagnon, whom I met with this morning, is considering his legal options. In the meantime I said that I would endeavour to meet with your client so that we have some idea of the strength of the assertions Georgina Hart is going to make in her story. Does that sound unreasonable?'

Jennifer paused for thought.

'I will have to consult with him,' she said eventually, 'but I would not have thought so, no. If Georgina Hart is going to publish his allegations, she has presumably persuaded him to go on the record. In that case the original reason for requiring you to sign an NDA is no longer applicable.'

'Yes,' I replied. 'The whole purpose of that was to maintain his anonymity if I wished to use his material.'

I hesitated for a moment. 'So you'll ask him?'

I sensed the slight nod as Jennifer replied, 'I will ask him.'

'Soon?'

'I will ask him soon.'

***

Kate arrived back from I know not where shortly after my call with Jennifer, and I told her about the day's developments over a late lunch, starting with my early meeting in Newark.

'I feel very guilty,' she said morosely, looking up at me from her plate for reassurance. 'If I hadn't talked to your Georgina things would never have got this far.'

'Your Georgina' was shorthand between us now, and I no

longer took offence from it: I think most couples evolve such 'entre-nous' phrases. Nonetheless, the sentiment was true.

'I kept you out of it, don't worry,' I said, though I was indeed concerned that this aspect would eventually be revealed. I knew Kate was too. She smiled wanly.

'So, what now?'

I shrugged. 'Meet with this guy if I can. Do my best to find out the line he's spun to Georgina. Maybe try and have another chat with her once I know more. And feed whatever I find into Jazzer so he can crank up his lawyers.'

'I don't think they'd have much of a case,' replied my legally qualified wife dubiously. 'Maybe invasion of privacy – Rowena's privacy – but that'll mean the complaint will have to come from her, not Jazzer. And probably after the article has been published, which rather negates the point.'

'And it all depends what Jennifer's client says anyway,' I added. Kate nodded.

'Yes. If he'll talk, you need to speak to him pronto.'

After lunch I checked my emails, as was my custom whenever I was working from home. The only one of any substance was from Jennifer Acland, who had clearly followed up on our conversation immediately.

The gist of it was that her client, who was called David Learmont, had indeed met with Georgina at her request, although he had been unaware of her profession and had opened up to her only because she was Michael Sweetman's niece. He did not favour a meeting between us, but would take a call from me, though with no guarantees that he could or would answer my questions. Eleven the next morning was suggested. Jennifer asked me to confirm that I could make myself available then, and gave me a number to call, with strict instructions that I was not to do so at any other time, or her client would refuse to talk at all.

I replied swiftly accepting the 11 am telephone appointment, and settled back to think.

I was lacking a lot of information, notably David Learmont's attitude to the forthcoming article. He sounded thin skinned, defensive and prickly. It wasn't clear whether he was glad to have talked to Georgina, but my working supposition, given his inherent sensitivity about his privacy, was probably not. This might give me some leverage when we spoke, but I was not at all sure how I would confirm it, nor how I would use such information if it was true.

I decided broadly that I would aim either to enlist David Learmont as an ally against the publication of Georgina's article, or to entice him to part with sufficient information to allow me to sow doubt in her mind about the wisdom of her intentions. It would be very difficult to prepare given that I knew so little about him as a personality.

So I'd have to do what had been necessary many times in my business career: play it by ear.

***

It's faintly intimidating calling anyone you don't know, even if they're supposedly expecting the call, so I wasn't much looking forward to 11 am the next day. But I'd had to do plenty of cold calling in business, which is much worse, so I picked up the receiver in a hopeful frame of mind.

'Hello?' said a reedy, middle-aged voice, after the phone had rung five or six times.

'Mr Learmont, good morning,' I replied as positively

as I could. 'We have a call now I believe? Arranged by your solicitor, Jennifer Acland.'

'Oh yes,' said the voice, with peevish unenthusiasm. This wasn't going to be easy, I thought.

'Well, as you may have heard a journalist called Georgina Hart is about to publish an article as a result of having spoken to you.'

'I didn't know she was a journalist,' replied the voice flatly.

'Can I ask how you came to be talking to her at all?'

'She rang me up. I'd never heard of her. I don't like unsolicited calls. I was about to put the phone down. Then she mentioned Michael Sweetman.'

'Whom you believe was your father?'

'He was my father; there's no doubt at all.'

Irritated; I'd annoyed him. Move on.

'So you must have been her mother's nephew, since she was Michael Sweetman's sister. Which makes you Georgina Hart's cousin.'

There was a long pause: he didn't seem to have considered this. 'I suppose so, yes.'

'What did she want to talk to you about?' I asked.

I could sense his impatience, though it was a perfectly fair question.

'She told me about the matching letters.'

'Between the ones she'd given me and the ones I got from General Montagnon?'

'Yes.'

'Do you know how she found that out?'

I did, of course.

'I have absolutely no idea, and even less interest,' came the prickly reply.

'So as to your involvement in this whole issue…?' I began.

'My parents didn't tell me I was adopted till just before my mother died, in 1988. It shocked me deeply, but I didn't do much about it till my father died in 2000. I mean my adoptive father. It would have upset him.'

'And somehow, quite separately from Georgina, you became aware of the Montagnon connection?'

'I did. After long research.'

'Did you outline that research to Georgina?'

'Broadly, yes.'

'And why did you want to speak to me under non-disclosure terms?'

'Before I spoke to Georgina Hart I was simply interested in finding out more about my birth family. Once it was apparent that my father and Giles Montagnon were love rivals we both became convinced that the death of Michael was suspicious. I still believe that. I thought that speaking to you might be a way of getting that information out there. That man was no hero, which is what everyone makes him out to be. But I didn't want to reveal my source, and…'

There was a long, thoughtful silence.

'What?' I said.

'My wife's family don't know I'm adopted,' said David eventually. 'I don't want them to. But I suppose it will all come out now.'

'And I presume the name of your original informant about the Montagnon connection will come out too?'

'Probably,' David replied bitterly, 'even though he asked me not to reveal it. I told that wretched woman everything. I thought she was only interested for private family reasons, like me. She's very persuasive.'

I knew it. I also knew when to push my luck.

'So will you tell me now who it was?' I asked.

'It was the regimental padre,' David replied quietly. 'He conducted my father's wedding, and was nearby when he died. Nick Carson.'

CHAPTER FIFTEEN

Kate was loitering in the kitchen suspiciously close to my study door when I entered after the call, seemingly putting away the last of a load of crockery from the dishwasher.

'So?' she said disinterestedly. It didn't fool me.

'She tracked him down, as we suspected,' I said. 'Almost certainly after talking to you.'

Kate winced. 'What's he like? David Learmont?'

'Hard work. Didn't want to talk to me, but the solicitor probably advised him to. Basically he became suspicious about Giles's role in Michael's death once he had spoken to Georgina.'

'How did he know about the Montagnon connection anyway?' replied Kate. 'That's definitely something you can't pin on me.'

'From the padre, apparently. Nick Carson. Whom he says married Michael and Rowena, and also spoke to Michael not long before his death. Perhaps they discussed the possibility that Michael was being deliberately exposed to danger by Giles.'

'Nick Carson didn't tell you any of that though, did he?' said Kate.

'He didn't not tell me any of it, either,' I countered.

She paused with a child-like frown on her face; her jaw set. I've always loved that look.

'Of course, those damn letters made David suspicious. So he opened up to Georgina when she contacted him.'

'And then of course she had her story,' I said, finishing her sentence. 'Yes, that's about the size of it, I think.'

'How did she know about David?'

'No idea,' I replied. 'But she's an investigator. It's hardly surprising.'

Kate looked grim, and now I reflect back upon it, determined as well.

'I'll stop her,' she said. 'It's my fault.'

'Yes, darling,' I said absently, and thought no more about it.

How much more bloody patronising can a husband get?

***

Not taking Kate's assertion seriously, I decided that I'd have another try at stopping Georgina myself, our less-than-satisfactory meeting a week or so before notwithstanding.

I mulled over the situation after lunch as I walked the dogs, and even discussed it with them: I sometimes do that to clarify my thoughts, and the great thing is that they always agree with me. We concluded that I had nothing to lose, and I called Georgina's mobile from my study on return.

Georgina answered straightaway, but I could hear that she was driving, which is never promising in terms of meaningful conversations. That said, she knew who I was, so she must have entered my number in her phone, which was at least a minor positive.

'Hello Dom,' she said. Neutral. Guarded.

'Hello,' I replied.

'What?' she interrupted, before I could say anything else.

'I just wondered if you'd had any further thoughts about the wisdom of proceeding with this article of yours?'

'I've made that decision, so no, I haven't given it any further thought at all,' she said, rather aggressively. But I knew that this was often a cover for uncertainty, so I decided to try to leverage that.

'I spoke to David Learmont,' I said.

'Thrill a minute, isn't he?' Georgina replied, in an unpleasantly sarcastic tone I hadn't heard before.

'Well, you're not flavour of the month with him, let's put it that way,' I said. 'He thinks you tricked him into opening up to you; he's worried that his adoption is going to become known to his in-laws, and he's also concerned that his informant is going to be revealed publicly. He made a promise that would never happen.'

'Nothing he said was off the record,' Georgina replied.

'He didn't know you were a journalist,' I responded. 'You were long-lost family to him. Naïve maybe. But understandable.'

'Well I'm sorry. But ultimately what I'm going to write is true. That's what investigative journalists do.'

'And no consideration for the feelings of General Montagnon or his mother?'

'It's the truth, for God's sake. Sorry Dom, I've got to go.'

I looked ruefully at my phone, sighed, and made the second call I'd decided upon.

Nick Carson sounded quite pleased to hear from me, right up until the moment I mentioned David Learmont.

'How do you know him?' he asked sharply.

'I've never met him. Spoke to him for the first time in my life this morning, on the phone. He explained to me that it was you who told him about the death of Michael Sweetman.'

'Whom he believes to be his father,' said the priest. 'I know. That's almost certainly true.'

'And you didn't tell him that Giles was responsible for his father's death?'

There was a pause.

'Look, he was looking for evidence to support a pre-formed theory. He may well have taken inferences from what I said, but I certainly did not tell him that.'

'How did you meet him?'

The old man hesitated. 'He was seeking out people who knew his father. I had married his parents, so obviously he was keen to meet me, and he found someone who could point him in my direction. He was persistent. I told him what I could, and of course Giles came up. I think he has a right to know.'

'Meaning you didn't tell him everything?'

'I did not want to reveal all aspects of the story, since he was Michael's son.'

'So you told him a version of the truth to spare his feelings?'

'Something like that. He has persuaded himself that Giles is to blame.'

'Was he?' I asked bluntly.

Nick Carson sighed.

'There is more to this story than meets the eye. If your investigative journalist is pedalling David Learmont's theory, she is barking up the wrong tree.'

I paused to reflect.

'How did Michael Sweetman die?' I asked.

'Artillery fire. Or it may have been mortar – it matters not which.'

'That's pretty random. Giles surely can't be blamed?'

'I do not wish to say any more,' said the clergyman. 'Good afternoon.'

I could sense the vexation in his voice before the receiver was quietly replaced.

***

I reported by phone to Charlie, and it wasn't more than an hour before he was back on the line asking if I could make it over to Newark again the following morning to confer with him, Jazzer and Sam. At least I'd been asked this time rather than peremptorily summoned, so I accepted with as much grace as I could muster.

When I arrived they wanted to hear it all again. Jazzer seemed oddly detached from the apparent revelation that he had a half-brother who had been adopted at birth, though both Charlie and Sam were clearly surprised. However, they downplayed this in the face of Jazzer's imperturbability. Then we turned to Georgina Hart.

'She's going to publish,' I said. 'I've tried talking to her. No dice.'

'Bloody woman,' said Sam contemptuously, in the sort of tone one simply wouldn't use today.

'Well – she believes it's the truth…' I began.

Jazzer raised his hand. 'Believes what's the truth? Let's be clear about this, Dom.'

'All right. She believes your father engineered her uncle's death. Is that clear enough?'

Jazzer puffed out his cheeks. 'Quite unprovable, surely?' he said.

'What did your lawyers say?' I asked him.

'They dressed it up in all sorts of fancy words to justify the ridiculous amount they charged me,' he replied, 'but the essence is that until she publishes there's not much we can do. And once she does, it's too late: my father's reputation will be traduced.'

'A man like that; a bloody hero…' grumbled Sam.

'The thing is, I think there's more to it,' I interrupted.

'What do you mean?' said Charlie.

'Nick Carson told me he didn't tell David Learmont the whole story, to spare his feelings. And it's the Learmont accusations that Georgina's going with.'

There was a pause.

'Well, what is the whole bloody story?' exploded Jazzer, glaring around at all of us. 'Why won't the wretched padre tell us? At least we might be able to sow some doubt in the mind of the Hart woman if we knew that.'

It was a good question, to which I did not know the answer, though no doubt Nick Carson had his reasons. I said without much enthusiasm that I'd try and talk to him again, but with scant chance of success.

'If there's anything more tell him that we need to hear it,' directed Jazzer forcefully. 'Damn it, I'll go and see the wretched man myself if I have to.'

There was a bit more to and fro, but nothing meaningful, and broadly speaking on that rather unsatisfactory note we broke up.

And as normal, I debriefed Kate as soon as I got home. She didn't seem that interested.

CHAPTER SIXTEEN

The next day was a Saturday, and having put the dogs in kennels Kate and I took some time out to attend my nephew Ben's marriage in North Yorkshire, where his intended lived. It all went off splendidly: the bride looked radiant, there was an excellent party in the evening, and it was late on Sunday afternoon before we arrived back home, tired but happy with the elation that only a top-notch wedding can impart. I hadn't thought about the events of 1944/45 and their present day ramifications for over forty-eight hours, and was all the better for it.

On Monday I had something on in London, and caught an early train from Market Harborough, falling in with several unfortunates who were still making that City commute on a daily basis, which luckily I was no longer obliged to do. It was good to see them again though, plus the meeting of charitable trustees in which I was involved didn't drag on for too long, and culminated in a very tolerable lunch at Boodles with amenable companions, so I was in high good humour by the time I got home just before 5 pm.

There was no sign of Kate, but that didn't concern me unduly since I've never been one of those paranoid individuals who insists on knowing where their wives are every instant of the day: to my wife's astonishment, her close friend Amelia had once found a tracker on her car (or rather the garage had, whilst servicing it). Kate had never viewed Amelia's husband in the same light since, and nor had I. We didn't have that sort of relationship, so I wasn't remotely worried.

I took the dogs out for a stroll on a lovely evening, and reflected contentedly upon my good fortune. Fate is easily tempted in such circumstances.

I was marginally concerned by about 6 pm: no more than curious really. I didn't want Kate to think me a worrier though, so put on the evening news and told myself I'd call her once the half hour bulletin was over. But in fact she called the landline just as I was settling down.

'Dom – darling: thank God,' she began, and then stopped with what sounded like a sob. Not like my level-headed Kate at all.

Something was clearly terribly wrong, and I felt the hairs on the back of my neck rising.

'What is it? What's the matter?' I asked her urgently.

There was open sobbing on the other end of the line.

'When you're ready – take your time,' I said as calmly as I could, which probably wasn't very.

'She's dead,' Kate blurted out.

'Slow down: who's dead?' I replied. I sensed the answer even before Kate told me.

'Georgina. I found her. She was shot.'

'What? That's unbelievable. Where…?'

'At her house – listen; I'm with a policeman. He'd like to speak to you.'

I was dumbstruck. 'Of course.'

'Mr Dominic Mallory?' asked an authoritative voice.

'Yes – that's me,' I replied, dazed. 'What's going on?'

'I am Detective Inspector Ian Webster of Towcester CID,' the voice replied. 'I'm afraid your wife has been involved in something extremely unpleasant. She appears to have discovered the body of a murder victim.'

There's no easy reply to something like that: certainly my 'Are you quite sure?' was entirely inadequate.

'Quite sure,' said the detective calmly. My head was spinning.

'Does she need a lawyer?' I asked eventually.

'No – we have asked her some preliminary questions under caution; she voluntarily gave up that right, though as our inquiries progress she can of course call on one at any stage. We don't think it'll be necessary though.'

'So she's not involved in this crime?'

'Our inquiries are still ongoing, but at this stage we do not believe so, no.'

'And – can you tell me any more about the circumstances?'

The detective hesitated.

'Look – Mr Mallory,' he began. 'Your wife is not under arrest, but we do not think it is right that she drives home having had such a severe shock. Would you be able to come and pick her up from Towcester police station? It's less than an hour's drive from you. We can fill you in on what we know then.'

'Yes – of course. Straightaway.'

'And Mr Mallory,' the policeman continued. 'This is a murder inquiry. For the moment I would prefer you not to discuss it with anyone else. That is an instruction; not a request.'

'I understand,' I replied. 'But to be quite clear – the victim is Miss Georgina Hart?'

'That is so,' replied Inspector Webster, evenly. 'You knew her, I understand?'

'I do. I mean I did. I'll be there within the hour.'

***

I don't know about Kate, but I probably wasn't in much of a fit state to drive myself. My mind was in turmoil as I set off towards Northampton, which I would have to pass through en route to Towcester.

I couldn't work out what Kate was doing at Georgina's house anyway. As to who would want to kill her – unless there was some issue in her private life of which I was wholly unaware, it must surely be linked to the article she was shortly due to publish.

So, who would that put in the frame?

My brain went through endless gyrations: any number of people had good reason not to want Georgina's article to see the light of day. I did not think it would be that difficult for a competent police investigation to establish who had the opportunity as well as the motive. But further speculation would be fruitless until I knew more about the circumstances of the murder.

I flew down the A43 once south of Northampton,

touching 90 mph or more at times: there was only one speed camera on that road before you reach Towcester (there still is), and I knew where it was.

As I turned into the car park at Towcester police station I immediately spotted Kate's Volvo 4 x 4 parked up at the end of a line of police cars. It was surrounded by police evidence tape: a surreal sight. I had arrived within forty minutes, which may have raised the odd police eyebrow, though given the rather more important matters at hand they were good enough not to mention it.

The desk sergeant was expecting me, and within two minutes of my arrival DI Webster had arrived in reception. He was rather what one would envisage a Detective Inspector to look like: a bit younger than me, dark haired, slim, suited and obviously capable. I liked him on sight.

After we had shaken hands he led me through a door to an interview room on the left, all Formica tables and chairs. And there was my darling Kate, sat across a table with a policewoman, sharing a pot of tea. Her face was puffy from weeping, and she looked exhausted, but she seemed to have regained her equilibrium a little, and was smiling at something the policewoman had just said as I entered.

Her chair flew back, and she was in my arms in a moment; tears beginning afresh.

'Dom; Dom; I'm so sorry,' she began.

'Shh,' I said. 'Sorry for what? You haven't killed anyone.'

'Just that I thought I could sort it out. You know – I let the cat out of the bag in the first place. Her business card was on your desk, with her home address. I called her; no answer. So I thought – why not just drive over, and persuade her to drop it? It's not that far.'

The two police officers looked on unfazed: I guessed they'd covered this ground with her already.

'Well that's fair enough, isn't it?' I said, trying to comfort her.

She broke my embrace and shook her head vigorously.

'No – it's not bloody fair enough. I deceived you.'

'How?'

'When you came back from that meeting with Jazzer and the others on Friday. You were so downbeat. I knew you'd be in London today. I decided to sort it out without telling you.'

'I might have advised against it, but I'm not angry with you,' I said. 'You were trying to help. Would you mind telling me what you discovered when you got to Georgina's house?'

'Have you ever been there?' she asked, surprisingly sharply.

I saw the police officers take an interest, though I was unconcerned, as I could account for my movements right up until 5 pm. We all sat down at the table.

'No,' I answered truthfully. 'Never.'

'Well, it's pretty isolated. A cottage by itself on a big rural estate. I deliberately got there about two-thirty to avoid lunchtime. I was quite nervous, having only ever spoken to her on the phone.'

'Understandably,' I said.

Kate paused for thought.

'As I told these guys,' she said, 'I saw her car outside, a Golf. Frankly I'd have been relieved if it hadn't been there. But it was, so I had no excuse to turn tail. I parked up and knocked on the door.'

I waited for her to continue, her brow furrowed in thought.

'I was pretty hesitant. But the thing is – the door was ajar. So it sort of opened after I knocked. After that I stuck my head around it and said "hello".'

'And?'

She began to pucker up, but controlled herself.

'The first thing was – I smelt gunpowder. Very faint, but I know the smell; I've been pheasant shooting often enough with you. I knew what it was straightaway. But I had no idea—'

'What did you find?'

'You enter the cottage straight into the drawing room. The kitchen is off that to the right. I sensed something was wrong, so I went inside, very tentatively, calling out her name.'

'And that's when you found her?' I asked.

Kate nodded, grimly. 'She was on her back, in the kitchen. White top. There was a lot of blood. She was obviously dead; eyes wide open: I didn't have to check to see that. I used the phone in the drawing room to call 999.'

'And you didn't call me too?'

She shook her head. 'I did try. No answer. Then the police arrived; they were very quick.'

I pulled my mobile out. There was indeed a missed call from a strange number at 2.44 pm – just about when I'd been finishing my excellent lunch. I'd turned my mobile off, and hadn't checked it since.

DI Webster stepped in.

'Shotgun – a single shot, from close range. She stood no chance.'

'But why?'

'That is what we would like to talk to you about, Mr Mallory. Your wife has given us some of the background as she understands it. But you will obviously know a great deal more.'

I accepted this with a nod, then paused.

'Look, Inspector. My wife is exhausted, and has been through a terrible experience. I would like to get her home, and also to gather my thoughts. It is getting late. How would it be if we reconvene first thing tomorrow morning to discuss all this? We can pick up my wife's car at the same time.'

The Inspector reflected for a moment and came to a decision; he looked tired himself.

'Happy with that. But if you are in agreement, I'll willingly drive your wife's car back to you. My Sergeant can follow, and take me back to the station afterwards. It might be helpful to see you both on home territory, so to speak, and you'd be able to show us these letters Mrs Mallory has been talking about. We have the address.'

'Thank you; agreed. Shall we say 10 am then?'

***

Kate said nothing as she belted up. I knew she would talk when she was ready, and squeezed her briefly on the thigh as the car nosed out of the police car park. She gave a tight little smile.

'I really am sorry,' she said briefly, as we reached the outskirts of Towcester.

'Well – nobody expects to stumble into a murder,' I replied. 'I'm just relieved you didn't get there any earlier. You can't have missed him by much.'

'If it was a he,' Kate responded. 'No physical strength needed to do that.'

I glanced across at her briefly as I joined the A43 via the Towcester roundabout. 'Any theories?'

She shook her head. 'Not really. There are only a limited number of people who knew about Georgina's story. And who on earth would feel strongly enough about it to kill? It should be straightforward to establish who had an alibi this afternoon and who didn't. It just seems so bloody rash.'

'Or desperate.'

'Yes. Or desperate.' She fell silent.

'Unless it's nothing to do with the wretched Sweetman business at all,' I suggested after a couple of minutes. 'Maybe she just had a jealous lover or something? A stalker.'

'Maybe,' said Kate unenthusiastically: she clearly didn't think much of this idea. 'I'm sure the police will check.'

'Well, what do you think then?' I asked.

'I just don't know, Dom,' she said quietly. 'I only know that I can't believe what's happened. Poor woman. What a nightmare.'

After a minute or so I looked across at her again: she was fast asleep, and remained so till we drew up at home about forty minutes later. Even then I had to wake her.

I poured us both a stiff whisky as soon as we got in, and Kate toddled upstairs to drink hers in the bath: she wasn't hungry. I can't say I was surprised given what she'd seen earlier in the day, but I was disappointed: the shock had affected me differently; adrenalin was coursing through my veins, and I wanted to hear every last detail.

But that would have to wait until morning. I had a second whisky and rustled up a pretty poor omelette, all the while mulling over the scarcely believable events of the day, and then followed my wife upstairs.

She was in bed already, and out for the count. I treated myself to a bath too, and joined her within twenty minutes, setting the alarm for 7.30 am.

After brief reflection about what the morrow would bring, and savouring my overwhelming relief that Kate was safe, I too fell very quickly asleep.

***

When I stirred, I could sense Kate wide awake beside me. It was just before 7.30 am, so I turned off the alarm on my phone. I gave her a quick peck on the cheek, and went downstairs to feed the dogs and make her morning coffee.

She was half dressed by the time I returned, and looking unnaturally pale.

'Don't worry,' I told her. 'We've got nothing to hide, have we? I'll just tell them the truth.'

'I know,' she said. 'I just can't get that vision out of my mind. I've never seen a dead body before – even when Daddy died, I didn't go to the undertakers when they laid him out.'

I gave her a brief hug. 'I'm sorry you had to see that.'

'It's all very well them saying don't tell anybody,' said Kate as she broke free to finish buttoning up her shirt. 'But this is going to be in the papers – on the TV. The radio. We can't hush it up forever. And then the press are going to want to talk to me too…'

I could sense her wobbling. 'We'll ask the police. Take their advice,' I said.

'Do I need a lawyer?' Kate said. 'I think it would be prudent.'

'Let's get this session over,' I replied. 'We'll decide then. It would probably be sensible at least to get one stood by.'

'Who?'

I shrugged. 'Maybe that woman I sat next to at the Frobishers,' I replied. 'Lois whatever her name is, she knows some of the background. Seemed pretty clued up. I liked her.'

Kate nodded. 'OK. Not her husband though – awful bore.'

After that it was a long old wait till 10 am, and I cursed myself for not asking the police to come earlier. We decided not to speculate. Kate wondered if she would be allowed to sit in on my questioning, which I thought was unlikely. She pouted, and started laying out some coffee and biscuits.

At around 9.40 am Jazzer rang. I can't recall what it was about now, but I was forced to brush him off pretty brusquely. I said something to the effect that it wasn't a good time, and I'd call him back later.

At exactly 10 am the dogs began to bark. The police had arrived.

CHAPTER SEVENTEEN

I emerged from the house as DI Webster was parking Kate's Volvo in our yard. Following him was an unmarked maroon Vauxhall saloon from which another man emerged; a plain clothes police officer I assumed. I hadn't seen before.

I sensed Kate close behind me as I moved forward to greet the visitors.

'Good morning, Detective Inspector,' I said, extending my hand to him as he turned from the car.

'Good morning, sir,' Webster replied, shaking my hand briefly, before turning to his colleague. He looked much refreshed from the previous night.

'May I introduce Detective Sergeant Pearson?' he said, handing me the keys to the Volvo at the same time.

Pearson was burly, to put it kindly, with the macho type of moustache I generally disliked. He nodded briefly, and looked around to take stock of his surroundings. I could see him computing: money.

'Can I offer you both some coffee?' asked Kate, brightly.

The Inspector nodded his assent, and the two policemen followed us into the kitchen. As Kate poured, I asked how he wanted to proceed. It was as I expected.

'At this stage, sir, we have no further need to talk to Mrs Mallory; we just want to question you on what you know of the background to this crime. So if you wouldn't mind, ma'am…'

'Of course not,' said Kate, in the overly gracious manner which I knew meant that she minded a great deal. 'I'll be next door if you need me.'

She disappeared quietly into my study with her coffee, giving me a tight little smile as she went.

The three of us looked at each other, and Pearson ostentatiously drew out his notebook. He still hadn't said a word.

'Now sir, can you please tell us how you were acquainted with Georgina Hart?' said Webster.

'Well, as I'm sure my wife has told you—' I began. Webster raised his hand.

'She has. We would like to hear it from you.'

I wondered briefly how to summarise this at tolerable length.

'I met her twice,' I said eventually. 'I have been asked to write a history of Prince Rupert's Horse in the years 1944 and 1945 – the Regiment in which I once served.'

'As an officer?' interrupted Pearson, in disapproving fashion. I was beginning to get a measure of the man.

'Yes – as an officer,' I replied, staring him down. 'Does that make a difference?'

Pearson did not reply, but continued writing laboriously in his notebook.

'And remind me, how did this lead to you meeting Miss Hart?' asked Webster.

I was sure he knew perfectly well, but clearly he wanted me to spell it out for Pearson's benefit.

'She responded to a request I put out for anyone who had any artefacts from that time,' I replied. 'She had some letters. From her uncle. And in fact to him as well.'

'Michael Sweetman – who died in March 1945,' said Pearson, as if this in itself was suspicious.

I nodded. 'Michael Sweetman.'

'And so…?' began Webster.

'And so I asked her to lunch: we met in a pub. She gave me the letters to study.'

Pearson was still writing.

'Now, correct me if I am wrong, but these letters appear to be the crux of the matter,' said Webster. 'Can you explain why that was so?'

I paused to take stock.

'Very possibly,' I said eventually. 'There were two sets of letters. One of them had been sent to Georgina Hart's mother, who was Michael Sweetman's sister. They are of no great import. The other set was from his wife.'

'So what?' said Pearson, rudely.

I thought for a moment.

'Wait here,' I said, and vanished into my study, where Kate raised an eyebrow archly at me as she leafed through a magazine.

The door was ajar, so I said nothing to her. It took me only half a minute to dig out the letters Rowena had sent her first husband, and to put them in a plastic sleeve. I handed them over once I had re-entered the kitchen; Webster looked at them without much interest, and then passed them to Pearson.

'Well, they don't say much, do they?' said Webster.

'That's not the point,' I replied. 'Look at these.'

I handed over the second sleeve I was carrying. Pearson perked up.

'It's the same handwriting,' he declared.

'It is,' I agreed. 'But they were not written to the same person.'

And so it all came out: the letters sent to Giles in the desert; Kate revealing the handwriting match to Georgina; Georgina tracking down Michael Sweetman's adopted son; the allegations that as the Regiment's Commanding Officer, war hero Giles Montagnon had deliberately exposed his love rival to danger; the intended *Daily Mirror* expose by Georgina Hart, investigative journalist.

'Is that sufficient reason to kill?' mused Pearson sceptically.

Webster was of course ahead of his colleague, having interviewed Kate the previous day.

'Tell Sergeant Pearson who asked you to write this regimental history,' he asked me.

'I was asked to write it by Lieutenant General Sir Jasper Montagnon,' I stated flatly.

Pearson looked on uncomprehendingly.

'The son of Lieutenant Colonel Giles Montagnon, against whom these allegations were being made,' said Webster smugly, enjoying his colleague's discomfiture.

***

The police spent another two hours with me, which was longer than I had bargained for: Kate too, who rather huffily departed to walk the dogs halfway through the interview having confirmed that she would not be needed 'today, at any rate'.

First they established my movements on the day, and since I'd been in Boodles at the time Kate called me just after discovering the body, and had plenty of witnesses to it if need be, this line of questioning didn't take long. Then we covered Jazzer, and Charlie, and David Learmont, and Nick Carson, plus peripheral characters like Mary, and Rowena, and Sam Lane. They were thorough, and took their time to understand how all these people fitted into the story, Pearson all the while taking his meticulous handwritten notes. I was impressed.

At the end of it all I asked if they would mind a couple of questions from me.

'No,' said Webster. 'I'll answer what I can.'

'First – is it possible that all this is irrelevant: a co-incidence? Maybe an old lover, or perhaps a stalker? Unrequited love? Maybe even a burglar?'

'We're looking at those possibilities,' confirmed the detective. 'Nothing substantive yet. In terms of burglary, there was nothing taken from the house, it seems – and opportunistic thieves don't usually carry shotguns.'

I nodded, and moved on.

'Secondly – all this is going to be in the public domain soon, if it isn't already. General Montagnon – all those others. I can hardly say nothing about it to them given that we've all been worrying about what Georgina Hart was going to publish – especially if it comes out that my wife discovered the body, as I'm sure it will.'

The two policemen looked at each other. Surprisingly, it was Pearson who answered.

'You can tell them what's happened. Also that we'll be in touch. Anyone who has a possible association with this crime is going to be interviewed. There is a very dangerous killer out there.'

'Thank you,' I said. 'And one more thing: you're probably not the right people to ask, but should my wife engage a lawyer?'

Webster sighed. 'Well, she was there, and not long after the murder. She has no alibi, and never pretended she did when questioned last night. Off the record, it's extremely unlikely she was involved, so unless you know something we don't I wouldn't have thought it was worth consulting a lawyer. What conceivable reason would Mrs Mallory have to do it?'

'None – and she just wouldn't, anyway,' I replied. 'Did you test to see if she'd fired a gun? Forensically, I mean? That would surely rule her out completely.'

I thought they both looked rather sheepish at this. Pearson simply shook his head.

'Well, thank you both, gentlemen,' I said, as we rose from the table. 'I won't say I enjoyed it, but I think you've got everything you possibly could out of me.'

'Thank you, sir,' said Webster. 'Interesting case. We don't get many like this.'

I thought this was rather overdoing the professional detachment given that someone had died a horrific death, but let it pass. I walked them to their car, and assured them as they got into it that Kate and I would both be available should they have any further questions. Then they headed off, Pearson driving.

Kate wasn't yet back from her dog walk. On a sudden impulse I headed for our safe under the stairs, to which I knew she had the combination, since it contained much of her best jewellery. It also contained the key to the gun cabinet, which was in a cupboard in my study.

I wasn't doing as much shooting anymore as I once did, but I still had a shotgun. With an unpleasant feeling of disloyalty, a few seconds later I found myself opening the cabinet.

The gun was there, upright and alone in the four-gun rack. I don't know what else I expected, but I knew for a certainty that Kate hadn't brought it back home the previous evening after her lengthy bout of questioning at the police station.

So it had never left the house, and I was relieved to know that. I was also surprised at how strongly I felt that relief.

***

It was very nearly 1 pm before Kate returned, and we discussed it all. She was still rather miffed that the police had not questioned her, and only slightly mollified when I pointed out that this in all likelihood was a very good sign: they were satisfied with her answers after doing so the previous day, and furthermore had informally advised me that she probably didn't need a lawyer.

'Do you believe them?' she asked, in a rather impatient tone, as if accusing me of foolish naivety.

'Frankly, yes I do,' I replied. 'You didn't do it, and you've explained why you were there. Someone had to discover her. It happened to be you, and you told them straightaway. They accept all that.'

Kate paused. 'I'd still rather we told a lawyer,' she said decisively.

I knew better than to argue given her legal background, and shrugged my shoulders.

'OK – I'll call Lois after lunch.'

Kate nodded briefly, and on that note she began rustling us up a salad of some sort. I thought we deserved a drink after a rather trying morning (though hardly so in comparison to Kate's experience the day before), and so fished a bottle of white out of the fridge and poured us both a generous glass.

Kate took a grateful sip – more of a gulp really – and flashed a glance up at me as she whisked the salad.

'Can we tell people? What about Jazzer?'

'We can tell him. And anybody else connected with all this. Also warn them that the police will be in touch. I'll get on with that this afternoon.'

'And other people? Friends? Like Amelia?' Kate asked.

I knew that she and Amelia told each other pretty much everything, and she'd be eager to share the dramatic experience she'd just gone through with her best friend.

'They didn't say not to,' I said dubiously. 'Though I suggest not quite yet. The murder will be common knowledge soon enough.'

Kate's expression indicated that this had not gone down well, and I was bracing myself for a biting retort when I saw her hesitate.

'Fine,' she said. 'I'll invite myself round for a coffee tomorrow morning.'

She looked up as if daring me to challenge her: instead I just nodded, and reached out to take the plate of salad she was handing me.

***

After lunch I got down to some calls. It was a Tuesday, and everyone was at work.

Lois was in a meeting, and would call me back. Jazzer's card allowed me to reach only his ADC, but after a brief explanation along the lines that I was a regimental contemporary the young Captain put me through, with the caveat that 'the General's next meeting is in twenty-five minutes, so please do not take up too much of his time, sir.'

He'd obviously explained who was on the line, as the next thing I heard was Jazzer's inimitable tones.

'Dom?' He was clearly curious.

'Yes – Jazzer, look I'm sorry to call you at work…' I began.

'No matter; I'm sure there's a good reason,' replied the General, and sat back to hear what it was.

'Look – I've got some rather dramatic news. Terrible news, really. You know that investigative journalist—'

'Georgina Hart?' interrupted Jazzer, warily. 'What of her?'

'She's been killed. Murdered.'

'Good God.' I was listening for any indication of false surprise, but Jazzer's reaction seemed entirely genuine to me. 'When? How?'

'She was shot dead at her cottage near Towcester yesterday afternoon. Shotgun.'

I sensed a moment of reflection on the other end of the line.

'No chance it was suicide?'

'No chance whatever. And furthermore – Kate discovered the body.'

'Kate – your wife? How on earth – what was she doing there?'

'She had some idea that she could persuade Georgina not to publish. Felt guilty; thought she was inadvertently the source of the story. I didn't know – I was in London.'

'And…?'

'And so when Kate got there, the door was ajar. She went in, and there was the body.'

'Christ – poor girl,' said Jazzer. I wasn't sure if he was referring to Georgina or Kate. He seemed utterly lost for words.

'Yes – look Jazzer,' I replied, 'the police questioned Kate last night, and they've done the same to me this morning. They are going to be in touch shortly with anyone else involved with all this, and they've given permission for me to let you know that. So you should expect them to make contact.'

'I quite understand,' said Jazzer. He was undoubtedly a cool customer. 'Who else?'

'Well – the Home Headquarters team. The priest. That supposed half-brother of yours. Maybe others: I don't know where their enquiries have led them.'

'And you've told them – precisely what?' asked Jazzer, calmly.

'I've explained the situation, much as we discussed the other day at Home HQ,' I said.

'So no doubt they think I've got a motive, to save my father's honour,' said Jazzer drily. 'Fortunately I think I should be able to put their minds at rest as to my whereabouts yesterday.'

I stayed silent.

'Did you get anything else out of that damned padre?' Jazzer continued.

'No – not willing to talk.'

'Hmm – I wonder how long he'll be able to sustain that line with the police?' mused the General. I sensed him switching back into military mode. 'Well – thank you for letting me know, Dom. Rum business. I'll call you this evening: my sincere sympathies to Kate. Must go – important budget meeting in ten minutes.'

CHAPTER EIGHTEEN

Bad news travels fast.

Jazzer must have used that ten minutes productively, because it wasn't much longer than that before Charlie Manning was on the phone.

It was Kate who picked up, and after her 'Hello Charlie' I recognised the rather distant tone she used with people she didn't particularly want to speak to, Charlie being one of my pre-Kate Army chums (and a particularly conservative one) she had never been close to him, and I hated to think of the mess he would be making of talking to the wife of a friend whom he probably knew had recently discovered a body. Charlie was inarticulate enough with women under the best of circumstances.

Kate's pained expression extended through thirty seconds or so.

'Anyway, here's Dom,' she said, without any further comment on whatever Charlie had been saying. She handed over the receiver to me with a grimace, raising her ever-expressive eyebrows.

'Charlie, good afternoon,' I said. 'I've a fair idea what this is about.'

I saw Kate miming to put the handset on speaker, and did so with a querying look whilst Charlie paused before responding.

'Yes – well; bad business,' he responded. 'Jazzer's just told me. Poor Kate.'

'Thank you. I could see that you were sympathising with her.'

Kate gave me a look of disdain and raised her eyebrows again.

'One does what one can,' replied Charlie pompously. Somehow I knew that was exactly what he would say. I waited to see what he wanted.

'Well – that's one problem we don't have to worry about now,' he said eventually. 'Georgina Hart.'

He sounded pleased. Kate and I looked at each other; shocked.

'Charlie – the woman has just been murdered,' I said, trying to control my emotions, which I suddenly recognised were nearer the surface than I knew. 'You just can't say that sort of thing.'

I sensed no embarrassment the other end of the line; Charlie stood his ground.

'True though, isn't it?' he said.

'I very much doubt it,' I replied, as coolly as I could. 'Do you think the *Daily Mirror* are going to take the murder of the author of their exclusive lying down? They'll put everything they have on this.'

This seemed to give Charlie pause for thought.

'Do you think so?' he asked, unhappily.

'Sure of it. And the police will put their A team on it too,' I said, twisting the knife. 'Too high profile a case not to.'

'When will it all come out?' asked Charlie.

'News tonight, papers tomorrow I expect,' I replied, with a confidence I didn't feel. 'The police will want to talk to you, you know.'

'What on earth for?' I sensed the alarm in his voice.

'Because you're wrapped up in it. So am I, so is Kate, so is Jazzer. It's inevitable. They've already spoken to us, Kate yesterday and me this morning.'

Charlie paused. 'Are you under suspicion?' he asked suspiciously.

'No Charlie, I don't think we are,' I replied. 'The police seem to be focusing in other directions.'

'I see,' Charlie responded uncertainly. 'Well – we'll speak soon I trust.'

The receiver clicked down before I had a chance to say goodbye.

'I don't trust that man,' said Kate firmly.

And in truth, suddenly I wasn't sure I trusted my old friend much myself.

***

The next day we had our meeting with the solicitor, Lois Laidlaw, and by then the story had broken.

I'd arranged the appointment straight after my call with Charlie, and her mobile went to voicemail, so I was forced to call the landline on the business card she had given me, which led only to her receptionist. I was put through swiftly enough once I made it clear that I was a close personal friend of Lois – which was stretching the truth a bit, but needs must.

I sensed a certain distance from Lois initially, as if she was expecting me to ask her another favour such as the trivial previous one, but she warmed up pretty quickly and agreed to an appointment first thing the next day once I outlined Kate's involvement in a bona-fide murder case. Those don't come along too often in rural Leicestershire.

She'd clearly read about the case in the papers by the time that Kate and I arrived at her Market Harborough office – though I'd only seen the *Daily Telegraph*, and there wasn't any meaningful coverage of Kate's role in that, the body having been discovered by a 'visiting friend'.

Lois asked someone to bring us a coffee apiece (she only took water herself), and it was very much her professional persona who talked to us rather than the cheery fellow dinner party guest I remembered from a few weeks previously.

'Now,' she said, once we were settled. She sounded like a schoolmistress talking to two recalcitrant children. 'Please tell me what happened. Everything.'

Kate and I looked at each other.

'Well, you remember I told you at the Frobishers that I was writing a regimental history?' I began.

'I do,' nodded Lois. 'And then there was something about a non-disclosure agreement, as I recall.'

'Yes – that was part of it. But not the start of it,' I confirmed.

'Then let's begin there, shall we? At the start of it,' said Lois.

It took us nearly an hour to set the scene: the background to me agreeing to write the history; the roles of Montagnon *pere et fils*; the quest for artefacts; the meeting with Georgina

Hart; Kate's slip-up in telling her about the matching letters; Georgina's identification and tracking down of David Learmont; the declined NDA; the somewhat opaque role of Nick Carson; Georgina's planned article, and finally my abortive attempt to persuade her to drop it.

All that established, Lois suggested we stop for 'a little break'. In truth I could use one by then for the obvious reason; Kate too. As I re-entered Lois's office before my wife I heard Lois asking her receptionist to defer her next appointment whilst ordering us both another coffee.

Once Kate had returned and our coffees had been delivered, Lois looked at us both in turn.

'So now we come to it,' she said quietly. 'The day.'

'Yes,' I said. 'I suppose we do. It was a very normal one for me until that evening. Travelled to London by train. Had a meeting, and a lunch. Then returned home. Kate wasn't there, but that wasn't unusual. Then she called. I spoke to the police, who explained that Kate had found Georgina dead. They suggested I come and fetch her from Towcester police station, which I did.'

'Plenty of people to vouch for you being at the lunch, no doubt,' said Lois. It was a statement, not a question. 'Which overlapped with the time of the murder.'

'Indeed,' I replied.

'And you had a more unusual day, didn't you?' said Lois rather patronisingly, turning to Kate. She struck me as one of those women who didn't much like other women, I thought, as she waited confidently for a response.

Kate explained what she had been trying to achieve. Lois raised an eyebrow sceptically.

'It sounds pretty stupid, and it probably was,' said Kate

defensively, 'but I felt I'd let Dom down, and I decided it was worth me driving down to try to persuade Georgina not to publish whilst he was in London. I thought the worst that could happen was that she would tell me to get lost.'

'Little did you know,' said Lois coolly. Kate lowered her eyes.

We went through the discovery of the body relatively quickly. Lois was much more interested in what the police had said and done once they arrived.

'They did not arrest you?' she asked.

'No,' said Kate. 'They were sympathetic from the start. Professional. I trusted them.'

'The police will generally only arrest if they strongly suspect someone of committing an offence, because an arrested person has certain rights,' said Lois. 'But if you find yourself in a situation like that, you should always call a lawyer.'

Kate shrugged helplessly, and I that sensed that she was close to tears. 'Surely that would imply I had something to hide? I didn't.'

'They questioned you?' asked Lois, ignoring Kate's retort.

'Yes – why I was there, how I knew Georgina: that sort of thing.'

'Did they say that you were under caution?'

'I don't think so – how would they do that?'

'It's usually done after you're arrested – you have the right to remain silent; you are not obliged to say anything, but anything you do say may be given in evidence: you know. It's on TV often enough.'

'No – they never said anything like that.'

'It sounds like they were trying to get close to you,'

observed Lois, with a lawyer's scepticism. 'To gain your confidence.'

'I think they were just doing their job,' I protested protectively.

'They did gain my confidence,' exclaimed Kate. 'They let me speak to Dom. They suggested he come and picked me up. They were entirely sympathetic. They drove my car back the next day.'

'And I thought they were very fair when they interviewed me then,' I said, backing her up. 'I even asked them if Kate needed a lawyer.'

'And I bet they said no,' said Lois, leaving me feeling uncomfortably naïve.

'Look, both of you,' said Lois suddenly, leaning forward. 'The police have to solve this high-profile case, and the awkward fact is that Kate hasn't got a definite alibi. So be very careful about trusting them too much.'

'Do you think I'm a suspect?' asked Kate, indignantly. She had definitely recovered some of her feistiness. 'What did I do with the bloody gun then?'

Lois paused.

'Personally I think it is most unlikely you are a suspect. But they need one, and the English legal system is adversarial, so if they put you in the frame it will be us against them. If they ask to interview you again, call me without fail. I will be there.'

***

We had only just got home when my mobile rang, just after Kate had headed straight out again for the birthday lunch of one of her girlfriends. It was the Salisbury solicitor.

'Mr Mallory,' she said once I had answered, 'this is Jennifer Acland. I am sure I do not need to explain why I am calling you. What terrible news.'

'Yes, it is,' I replied. Though the murder of Georgina Hart had now reached the media, Kate's involvement had not insofar as I knew. I saw no need to mention it.

'I have spoken this morning to my client, David Learmont,' she said, and paused for a reaction.

'Not the easiest of people to talk to,' I said.

She hesitated, perhaps reflecting upon the degree of professional loyalty she should demonstrate, and went for the neutral option before cutting to the chase.

'Well... I wonder if I might ask you a question?'

'Of course – I'll answer if I can. If it's not too intrusive.'

'I understand. Have the police questioned you at all?'

I sensed that it might become difficult to maintain my veneer of detachment if she pursued this line, but answered truthfully.

'Yes. Yesterday.'

'That seems very early. The murder was not then in the public domain. Were you aware of what had happened before they called you?'

I reflected briefly. It was either lie or come clean, and I had no reason to deceive Jennifer Acland. Checkmate.

'Can I take it that we are talking in confidence? Even as regards what you may tell your client?'

'Off the record, you mean?'

'Something like that, yes. I'll need your word on it.'

I sensed her thinking.

'Obviously my client's interests are my prime concern – but you may rely upon my professional discretion,' she replied.

'All right. My wife discovered the body.'

There was a silence of at least ten seconds. 'Goodness me. How dreadful for her.'

It was said calmly, but that was Jennifer's nature. She hadn't asked why Kate was there, and the sympathy appeared genuine, so I thought I should give the solicitor some context.

'Kate blamed herself for revealing the handwriting match, which led to Georgina tracking down David Learmont somehow, and everything that flowed from that,' I explained. 'I was in London. She decided to drive down to Towcester unannounced and try to talk her out of publishing.'

'I see,' said Jennifer Acland, and paused. She was clearly waiting for me to continue.

'Well – Georgina's car was there, at her cottage. Kate knocked on the door. It was ajar. She went in, and that's where she was. Shot dead. Kate could still smell the gunpowder.'

'Then I am very glad she did not arrive a little earlier,' said Jennifer, firmly.

'I can't stop thinking about that,' I said. And indeed I hadn't, for the last forty-eight hours.

'And the police have interviewed your wife, I take it?'

'Yes – she called them straightaway from the house. They arrived very quickly, and questioned her at the station. She thinks they have behaved admirably.'

'No lawyer present?' asked the solicitor sharply.

'Not you too,' I sighed. 'We're just back from meeting a local one, and she read us the riot act as well. But no harm done, I think. The police rang to tell me what had happened, and asked me to come and get Kate, which I did. The next day – yesterday – they drove her car back to us, which is nearly an hour, and questioned me too. Thoroughly professional.'

'You clearly have an alibi if you were in London. Equally, it would appear that your wife does not.'

'Not as such. But I am confident the police are not suspicious of her. And my shotgun is here. She definitely didn't bring it back with her.'

'So you checked?'

'Everyone would in the circumstances,' I replied somewhat uncomfortably.

'Any such weapon could have been used, of course,' Jennifer continued. 'No meaningful ballistics with a shotgun.'

I presumed she had some prior knowledge of firearms murders, and thought we were probably venturing a little off piste in discussing this level of detail.

'Was there a specific reason you called?' I said, getting back to the point.

'Yes indeed,' replied Jennifer, with a hint of apology in her voice. 'David Learmont is to be questioned by the police tomorrow. He appears to be extremely worried about it. Between us, and in confidence again, abnormally so.'

'If he's got nothing to hide then I'm sure you'll tell him just to answer the questions honestly,' I said. 'You'll be there, I take it?'

'Indeed I will,' replied the solicitor. 'I called to ask what you knew, and I am grateful for your candour in that respect. But I know considerably less about what is going to transpire tomorrow than I would like.'

***

The next call, barely five minutes later, was from Jazzer – brusque and to the point.

'Dom – sorry I didn't call back yesterday.'

'No matter.'

'The police have been in touch, as you said. They're interviewing me tomorrow. Offered to come to the office, but I thought not.'

'Understandable,' I replied. 'You being interviewed by the police would set tongues wagging in the MOD.'

'Well, the fact of the murder is common knowledge now,' said Jazzer. 'But as you say, it's probably best not to make a spectacle of the aftermath.'

There was a pause. I knew he would come to the point.

'The thing is…'

'What, Jazzer?'

'They're going to interview Mary too.'

'Reasonable enough, surely? Just routine. They're going to be at your house anyway.'

He paused again. 'And my mother. They want to talk to her as well.'

I hesitated, somewhat bemused by his downbeat tone, but came down on the same side of the fence as before.

'Look, Jazzer, it's hardly surprising,' I said. 'Rowena's central to all this. Wrote the letters to both your father and Georgina's uncle, for one. I'm sure they just want to establish the historical background to the killing whilst they're with you.'

Jazzer snorted uncertainly.

'Not really on. She's nearly eighty-four.'

'But in good shape, I understand?'

'Who told you that?'

It had been Charlie of course, and I was mulling over how to respond without dropping him in it, but Jazzer moved swiftly on anyway.

'I suppose she is, for her age. What's he like, this inspector? Webster, is it?' he grumbled.

'Yes – Ian Webster,' I responded. 'I found him very fair. However his sergeant – Pearson, I think he's called – not pro the officer class: you know the type. I was rather wary of him. Though professional enough.'

'Hmm.'

'It'll be fine, Jazzer. Expect them to be thorough.'

'Thanks Dom,' he replied, sounding flat. 'I'll let you know how it goes.'

The line clicked dead, and a vague sense of unease gripped me as I put my mobile down. I pondered the source of that feeling, and it didn't take long.

There was more to it from the Montagnon perspective than it seemed I knew.

CHAPTER NINETEEN

was still pondering this whilst I was out as normal walking the dogs after lunch, when I received another call. It was from a mobile number, and I didn't recognise it, so I answered cautiously, fearing a cold caller.

'Dom, it's me. Mary Montagnon,' said the voice the other end.

I hadn't needed the explanation; her quiet voice was unique, but I had never heard it so agitated.

'Hello Mary—' I began.

'Jasper told me last night – on the phone. He was in London. How utterly dreadful for Kate.'

Pretty dreadful for Georgina too, I thought, probably meanly. I confined myself to a simple 'yes'.

She clearly had something else to say, and I waited to hear what it was. There was an unnatural pause for a moment before she began to tell me.

'Look – Jasper told me the police would want to speak to him, and in the circumstances that seemed perfectly reasonable,' she began. And then hesitated.

'I agree,' I said, prompting her, and trying to keep an eye on Rosie at the same time, who had spotted one of her *bêtes noires* (or perhaps *gris*) – a squirrel. She was off and running.

'The thing is – they want to talk to me too. He didn't think they would. Made an appointment to visit, tomorrow.'

I knew this of course from my earlier call with Jazzer, but some instinct prevented me from mentioning it.

'That's OK, isn't it? Rosie, damn you…' I began, as the spaniel vanished through a hedge.

'Well the thing is – what on earth's going on there?' said Mary, as I broke into a trot.

'Spaniel. Young and disobedient. Go on,' I said.

'What I was going to say is – I'm really worried,' she said, miserably.

Rosie came back through the hedge, thoroughly pleased with herself, and began lolloping happily towards me. I stopped trotting.

'Why? This isn't *Midsomer Murders*. You must be able to give some explanation of your whereabouts, surely? And why on earth would you want to kill Georgina Hart?'

'Well, maybe I wanted to save the honour of the family name?'

'Come on Mary,' I said. 'That is hardly credible, and I'm sure the police are not interviewing you on that basis. It's just routine. If you were alone at home, then just say so.'

There was a long silence.

'The thing is, Dom,' she said in a timid tone I'd never heard before, 'it's not really my whereabouts I'm worried about.'

'Don't understand.'

'It's Rowena's. They're interviewing her too.'

'And…?'

'And she wasn't here on the day of the murder,' she said, and paused to await my reaction.

'Are you sure?' I replied.

'Perfectly sure. Her car was gone most of the day. She left her garage door open.'

'Have you asked her?'

'Yes – when I told her about tomorrow's interview. She just clammed up.'

I suddenly realised what she was telling me.

'You can't seriously suspect her?' I said in disbelief.

'I don't know what else to think, Dom. Jasper will be home tonight, and I'll discuss it with him. I thought maybe I'd say she was with me if we can't get a straight answer out of her…'

'I'm not sure why you told me this, Mary,' I said. 'There's nothing I can do to help. But let me give you one piece of very sound advice.'

'Please,' she said humbly.

'Don't whatever you do lie to the police.'

***

Kate arrived back at about four, and filled me in on some local gossip from her lunch as we had a cup of tea in the kitchen: the murder hadn't featured, as it wasn't local. Her own starring role was not yet known, so she hadn't mentioned it at all.

After a while though she could see that my attention was wandering, and she knew in what direction.

'Come on then,' she said, with a sigh. 'I'm trying not to think about this any more than I have to until they've caught the killer, but clearly you don't feel the same. What do you want to talk about? Let's have it.'

I looked at Kate to see if she was serious. She was.

'OK,' I said. 'Leaving aside the possibility that it was some random stalker, or a figure from her past – who do you think killed Georgina?'

She paused reflectively. 'I'm not sure we can leave those possibilities aside. But if pushed I would say – Charlie.'

'Charlie?' I said in disbelief. 'Why on earth would Charlie want to do it?'

'I don't like him – he's a stuffed shirt, and probably thinks he's averting some regimental scandal. Regimental honour: you know how much all that nonsense means to him.'

It was true that Charlie was a traditionalist in the oldest possible sense, and I pondered this.

'Plus he's a shooting man, isn't he? And he didn't sound remotely upset by the murder when he spoke to us: simply saw it as a problem solved.'

This was certainly true, I thought uncomfortably. Though if I'd done it, I wouldn't be revelling publicly in the consequences.

'I'm sure Charlie will have a perfectly good alibi,' I said airily, with a wave of my hand. 'Anyway – moving on. How about this: Mary suspects Rowena.'

Kate's eyes widened – bullseye; very gratifying. 'What…?'

I explained the background. Kate looked doubtful.

'Well it can't be her, can it? She's just got some secret she doesn't want Mary to know about. Maybe a secret lover.'

Her eyes flashed mischievously, and I laughed. It was good to see her smile again after the horrors of the last three days.

'You're right. Whatever it is, I'm sure Jazzer will get to the bottom of it tonight, before Rowena speaks to the police.'

∗∗∗

Jennifer Acland emailed later that evening, well after working hours. David Learmont would like to meet me – in fact he was asking urgently to do so. I presumed it was something to do with his police interview.

Boot's on the other foot now, I thought grimly. If he thought I was flogging down to Salisbury again just to see him after all his cloak and dagger nonsense he had another think coming.

Then I saw from the email that he didn't expect that. He would get a train to Northampton, Leicester, Rugby or Market Harborough as I preferred – and he would be most grateful if I was prepared to meet him before the weekend.

I couldn't do Thursday, I knew. But Friday was pretty clear, and I confess that I was intrigued. I checked the train timetable we kept on the pin board in the kitchen.

'Friday, Northampton, arriving 14.14,' I emailed. 'Leaves Euston 11.57. Eat on the train. Will pick him up.'

As the email swooshed away I wondered why I hadn't told Jennifer simply to have her client call me.

But as I well knew, some people just like to make life dramatic, and I supposed David Learmont was one of those.

∗∗∗

The next day, Thursday, I had a morning appointment in Leicester with my dentist. That evening, somewhat the poorer, I was due at a Livery Company Dinner (Drapers' – very fine) as somebody's guest: consequently I'd booked to stay overnight the Cavalry & Guards Club in Piccadilly, where I'd remained a member despite having left the Army sixteen years before.

Frankly I could have done without the whole occasion, but I knew I'd enjoy it once I got there, and I didn't want to let my friend down: it was a generous invitation. I was a little worried about leaving Kate alone after her recent shock, but she shooed me on my way – rather too enthusiastically I thought. Accordingly I took the 4 pm train down happily enough, albeit with a slightly numb mouth.

Jazzer rang barely after I'd got settled in my seat. You can't rely on mobile reception on those trains even now, and certainly couldn't in 2005, so it was a pretty hurried conversation. In short, he wanted to discuss the police interviews with his family that day, and if I hadn't been on the train no doubt we would have done so there and then, but I explained that I was en route to the Club. He was already back in London, and his flat wasn't far away, so we agreed to meet in Geoffrey's Bar for a drink at 6.30 pm.

I was in the Club by 5.30 pm, and had time for a quick bath before changing into my black tie and heading upstairs. I'd booked in the basement, where single officers and those without their wives tend to gravitate: it's cheaper, and Club lore has it that you meet a much better class of person down there.

It was a few minutes before 6.30 pm when I appeared in the bar, and Jazzer was passing the time of day with someone I didn't recognise who looked of about the same exalted seniority. He was dropped abruptly as soon as I appeared.

Jazzer headed outside to the terrace (much shabbier then than it is now), indicating forcefully with his head that I should follow. He didn't look back.

I tarried briefly to buy myself a Scotch, put it on my room bill and headed off to join him, declining a well-meant offer from a couple of acquaintances to have a drink with them as I passed by on my way to the far end of the terrace. I indicated with my eyes where I was heading, and they smiled their understanding as they registered my high-ranking companion.

Jazzer obviously wanted privacy: there was nobody within three tables of us.

'Lovely evening,' I said, as I approached.

Jazzer looked tired, and said nothing as I sat down.

'How did it go?' I ventured somewhat tentatively.

'Not well.' He took a big swig of his gin and tonic.

'What do you mean?' I was astounded.

'Oh – all right from my perspective of course; any number of people could vouch for where I was on Tuesday. And the police were thoroughly professional, as you said.'

'What, then?'

Jazzer paused reflectively.

'The others. Mary was home alone: nothing wrong with that, but apparently she made a bit of a meal of it when questioned. I don't think she's in the clear yet.'

'Just nerves,' I said, with as much reassurance as I could muster. 'They're not going to arrest her simply on the basis that she stayed at home all day unless they have a lot of other supporting evidence. I'm sure they don't.'

'Maybe not,' said Jazzer grimly. 'But that's not the half of it.'

I waited for him to continue.

'My mother – Rowena – won't say where she was, and she wasn't at home. She outright refuses.'

'But that's extraordinary,' I said. I took a sip of my own drink.

'It's more than that, it's actually suspicious,' said Jazzer. 'They are going to interview her again under caution tomorrow. I've had to warn off the family lawyer to be there. Bloody hell.'

He shook his head in disbelief.

'Well if she has an alibi, she'd better produce it,' I said.

'I've told her. She just tells me not to worry, and that she is not going to break a promise.'

'To whom?'

Jazzer shook his head: he clearly wasn't used to being so bluntly defied. 'God only knows.'

He took another large sip. 'And that's not all, Dom.'

'What?'

He looked up at me, and I was taken aback by the raw anguish in his eyes.

'I'm beginning to think there might be something in it. Maybe my father really did have Sweetman knocked off.'

I had no idea what to say.

'God knows I had my differences with the old bugger,' Jazzer continued, 'but ultimately he was a proper regimental war hero. I'd hate to think he was a murdering shit too.'

CHAPTER TWENTY

A s I knew I would, I thoroughly enjoyed the dinner at Drapers' Hall, and crawled into bed at the Club well after 1 am: not what I had planned, but in truth probably inevitable. Despite the bracing effect of a full English breakfast I was still mildly hungover as I checked out and took a taxi to St Pancras. I noticed a missed call from Charlie Manning on my phone as I settled into my seat, but decided it could wait given the lousy reception on the train. My *Telegraph* beckoned.

Kate greeted me cheerfully on arrival home an hour and a half later, issued me with a coffee, which I suspect she knew I needed, and said that Charlie had rung twenty minutes earlier: would I please call him as soon as I got in, as there appeared to be something wrong with my mobile? She had promised to pass the message on, and had now done so.

'Over to you, my darling,' she said sweetly.

I sighed, retreated to my study and dialled Home Headquarters.

'Regimental Secretary,' intoned Charlie, in his usual best

received English tone. I smiled. It's not a phrase that trips easily off the tongue, and as ever with Charlie it didn't come out quite right.

'Charlie, it's me – Dom. You've been after me,' I replied.

'Yes – better late than never,' he sniffed. I sensed displeasure.

'What? I'm not at your beck and call.'

'Look – Jazzer's in an awful tizz about his mother—'

'I know,' I interrupted. 'He told me last night.'

'I'm aware of that.'

'What do you want from me, then? Nothing I can do about it. Wherever she was on the day, Rowena needs to tell the police.'

'Do you think they really suspect her?' he asked in a low voice.

'I have no idea, Charlie,' I answered, somewhat brusquely. And I didn't.

There was a short silence on the end of the line, and I knew Charlie was building up to something.

'Look, Dom,' he began, plaintively. 'You know these coppers. Jazzer says you even like them. Couldn't you just ask, so I can set his mind at rest? The whole idea that Rowena was involved in killing this wretched harpy is obviously unthinkable.'

'Georgina Hart was not a wretched harpy, Charlie – that is a thoroughly disgusting thing to say,' I said, feeling the sharp burst of adrenalin that unexpected anger brings. 'She was an extremely nice person. I liked her.'

I could picture Charlie looking at his phone askance.

'She was about to instigate a regimental scandal, Dom,' he said in a disbelieving tone, as if that excused everything.

There were few greater sins in Charlie's book. I suddenly realised that whether there was actually such a scandal was entirely secondary to him; it was far more important that anything like that never saw the light of day.

'Have you actually met the investigating policemen yet, Charlie?' I said through gritted teeth.

'No. Half-two today. Me first, then Sam.'

'Then I suggest you ask them yourselves. On second thoughts, don't. You'll make yourself look even sillier than you already are.'

Charlie took this with remarkable equanimity.

'It's too late anyway, Dom. Rowena is being interviewed under caution now. That's why I wanted to speak to you earlier. So you could get a readout from the police beforehand.'

I sighed. So that was it.

'I wouldn't have called them on that basis anyway, Charlie. And they wouldn't have told me if I had.'

There was a pause, and I could hear Charlie breathing heavily on the end of the line. He was angry.

'You need to decide which side you're on, Dom,' he said eventually. 'This is the wartime reputation of Prince Rupert's Horse at stake. I always thought you were one of us. Prince Rupert's bloody Horse. Got that?'

The phone went dead, leaving me staring at my handset in astonishment.

***

There was an email from Jazzer a few hours later, headed 'My Bloody Mother', which should give you an indication of the sulphurous tone of its contents.

Essentially Rowena had denied all knowledge of the crime when interviewed for the second time by the police, but then had retreated to 'no comment' (on the advice of her lawyer it must be said) when asked to account for her whereabouts on the day of the murder. Jazzer didn't think the police seriously suspected her, but understandably they were not going to let her off the hook whilst she continued to stonewall them.

I sent back a sympathetic but neutral response, sat back, and vented my feelings.

'Hell's Bells' was my chosen exhalation, which was not a phrase I had ever used before (or indeed since).

Kate stuck her head around the door.

'Is that the best you can do?' she asked curiously.

I showed her Jazzer's email, waiting for the puzzled frown I loved so much.

'What on earth is she doing? Is she gaga?'

'Apparently far from it, according to Charlie,' I replied. 'Talking of whom…'

I told Kate of my rancorous recent conversation with the Regimental Secretary, and she leaned back smugly.

'Told you,' she said. 'He's my tip.'

I dismissed this lightly of course, but in truth I had been more shaken by Charlie's explosion than I was prepared to let on.

'Let's not jump to hasty conclusions,' I said. 'David Learmont is wrapped up in all this—'

'… And you're seeing him tomorrow,' replied Kate coolly, finishing my sentence for me.

***

They've done Northampton station up to quite a ritzy standard now, but it was still pretty basic then. I arrived in good time, and made my way to the barrier. It occurred to me as I did so that I had no idea what David Learmont looked like.

He wasn't difficult to pick out: tall; alone; green parka; thinning grey hair; gazing around nervously: he looked about sixty, which would of course be right if he was indeed Michael Sweetman's son. I called out to him and waved.

'David?'

He looked around on hearing his name and waved back, with a shy smile.

'Hello, Mr Mallory,' he said. 'Thank you for agreeing to meet me.'

'Dominic, please,' I replied, ushering him out towards the car park. 'It's no problem.'

There's a hotel I know just outside Northampton near the village of Creaton called Highgate House – I'd used it quite often before for discreet business meetings, so I planned to head there: it was only five miles or so. Once in the car I tried to make small talk, which generally I'm good at, but as I suspected David Learmont was no great conversationalist. He wasn't deliberately uncommunicative, just shy, but after a few stilted answers to my opening gambits I admitted defeat and lapsed into silence until we arrived at the hotel.

I led David inside, settled in a discreet corner table and ordered a pot of coffee. When it arrived I poured us both a cup, sat back and looked at him.

'Well – over to you,' I said.

He spread his hands expressively. 'This is a terrible business,' he began.

'Yes, it is,' I replied, and waited for him to continue.

'I understand your wife found the body,' he said, almost apologetically.

'She did. A great shock,' I said, and waited again.

'If I had not talked to Georgina Hart then Mrs Mallory would not have had that dreadful experience, because there would have been no murder,' he continued, and looked up at me for corroboration.

I took a sip of coffee and nodded. 'Very probably true.'

He looked anguished, and I was certain that the emotion was genuine. I felt sorry for him.

'Have the police interviewed you yet?' I asked, in an effort to move the conversation along.

'Yes. Yesterday.'

'And?'

'I'm not good at that sort of thing. Any sort of formal interview. I get self-conscious, and nervous,' David said. 'It probably wasn't very impressive from the police point of view.'

'Well, if you've got nothing to hide then surely there's nothing to be worried about,' I said, rather impatiently. 'Couldn't you just tell them where you were on Tuesday?'

He seemed to shrink, almost as if he was ashamed.

'I'm a widower. Retired now,' he said. 'I don't get out much.'

I shook my head, and must have looked exasperated.

'What?' he said.

So I explained that neither Mrs Montagnon had a cast-iron alibi either, and that the older one was being actively obstructive. David paused reflectively before replying.

'You mean my mother,' he said quietly.

'I suppose I do,' I admitted, embarrassed. I had forgotten.

There was another pause. When it became protracted I decided to take the initiative.

'What do you want from me, David?' I asked, as kindly as I could.

He looked up at me, his shyness self-evident, but there was underlying steel there too.

'I still believe Giles Montagnon was behind my father's death,' he said. 'Do you?'

I sighed.

'I really don't know, David.'

'So you aren't going to put it in your book?'

'It's a history, and one of an organisation I'm very fond of,' I replied. 'I'm certainly not going to publicise unsubstantiated tittle tattle which casts aspersions on it.'

It was too abruptly put. David took a sip of his coffee: the cup shook, and I could tell he was struggling to control his anger.

'Georgina Hart – my cousin – died because of that tittle tattle,' he said, with quiet bitterness.

I felt deservedly uncomfortable.

'Let's go back to how you met Georgina,' I suggested. 'Without that meeting, none of this would have happened. Nick Carson put her in contact with you, didn't he?'

'He did,' admitted David.

'Remind me why.'

'Well, I'd tracked Nick Carson down. He had nothing much to say. But when Georgina contacted him too – and I've no idea how she found him – he probably thought it was the right thing to do. We were cousins, as you pointed out, who apparently didn't know of each other's existence.'

We lapsed into silence, and for the first time I felt we were on the same team.

'The Reverend Nick Carson has a piece of this jigsaw which nobody understands,' I announced eventually.

'That he does,' said David. 'I came to the same conclusion myself. The main reason I am here is to ask if you know any more than I do. I thought it would be best to ask that face to face. Also I wanted to apologise in person for the part I played in what befell your wife.'

***

Kate was curious as to what it was all about once I arrived home, having dropped David back at the station. After I had filled her in on our discussion I passed on his apology.

'Not his fault,' she said quietly, 'but appreciated anyway.'

She lapsed into thought. 'What about this priest, Nick Carson?'

'He blanked me last time I tried to talk to him,' I replied. 'But I'm sure the police will have spoken to him by now.'

'Well he can't have done it, surely? Why would he?'

'I'm sure he didn't. And I can't believe he's yet another bloody person who can't explain where he was on Tuesday. No – this is something to do with the death of Sweetman. Something nobody else understands.'

'Except maybe Rowena.'

I gaped at her. That woman never ceases to astound me.

CHAPTER TWENTY-ONE

I called Nick Carson straightaway, but he didn't pick up, so I left a message on his answering machine (I don't think people used the term 'voicemail' then). After that I rang the Montagnon household, but since it was a weekday Jazzer was in London: I got Mary.

'Listen, I've had an idea,' I began, after our initial pleasantries. My wife eyed me sternly from her stool at the kitchen island.

'Well, it's Kate's idea really.'

'Yes...?' replied Mary, with polite unenthusiasm.

'You know Nick Carson, the padre?'

'I know who he is – but I've never met him,' said Mary. 'Have you?'

'I have, once, but that's not the point,' I said urgently.

Mary waited, and I could tell that she was disconcerted by my vigorous response.

'Look – what if Rowena went to see him?' I asked. 'They're the same wartime generation. I think they know more about this than any of us.'

'Why would she?' said Mary, dubiously. 'And even if she did, why would that be such a secret? Why not tell the police where she'd been?'

'I don't know. But Jazzer told me that she wouldn't tell them where she was because she refused to break a promise. So if they did meet, that infers the secrecy is at Nick Carson's behest.'

'I see what you mean,' said Mary hesitantly.

'Look – is Rowena there now? At her cottage?'

'I think so – wait,' Mary said. I pictured her moving to the window. 'The garage door is shut. She leaves it open when she takes the car out.'

'Will you go and ask her if she went out on Tuesday to meet Nick Carson?'

Mary hesitated.

'She's difficult, Dom…' I sensed Mary building up to a refusal. 'Look – Jasper's home this evening. He's commuting daily till all this blows over rather than staying in the flat. I'll definitely tell him what you think. Then he can decide what to do about it.'

She sounded very prim and 'Lady Mary'. I could sense her relief that she'd crafted herself an escape route. No point in me fighting it.

'OK. But I definitely think it's worth her being asked the question, Mary.'

'I understand. I don't think she'll answer dishonestly if Jasper asks her point blank.'

'Meanwhile I'll keep trying to talk to Nick Carson,' I said despondently. 'I don't even know if the police have spoken to him yet.'

I rang off thoughtfully, and decided I'd better provide

myself with a bit of insurance that the message would actually get through.

Whilst Kate waited, I summarised my thoughts in a few lines to Jazzer's personal email address.

***

I'd been mulling over my unfortunate conversation with Charlie Manning in the morning, and it appeared he'd been doing the same, because he rang me just after 6 pm. I could see from the number that he was at home.

'Hello Dom,' he began. I detected slight diffidence, and let him dangle for a bit.

'Hello Charlie,' I responded eventually, with some coolness. 'To what do I owe the pleasure?'

Kate's well-known 'distasteful' expression put in an appearance as soon as she knew who I was talking to, as I knew it would. I put the phone on speaker so she could listen in.

'Well – about earlier. Wasn't really on,' he mumbled.

I thought this was probably about as near an apology as I was likely to get, and though I wasn't really bothered by our little spat I didn't want Charlie to think I would routinely tolerate such behaviour.

'No. It wasn't,' I said.

'Well, I'm sorry,' he replied. He may even have meant it. There was a long pause.

'I've spoken to the police now,' Charlie said eventually. It was very low key – an attempt to engage me in a different conversation. A peace feeler, if you like.

'And – where were you when all this happened?' I asked.

'At Home Headquarters, of course,' said Charlie. He sounded mildly affronted to be asked.

I thought quickly. The crime had taken place on a weekday after all. Others worked there – Sam Lane and the Admin Officer, Amy; plus the Finance Manager, Anvi; sometimes others. So Charlie was surely in the clear. I caught Kate's eye, mouthed 'your bet' and gave her a thumbs down. There was no reaction, and I'm not sure she even noticed: she was listening intently.

'Did you pick anything else up?' I asked. 'About how the police are getting on?'

'No; I got the feeling they were a bit bamboozled by the whole thing,' replied Charlie. 'They're just country plods after all.'

I thought considerably more of Detective Inspector Webster than that, and told Charlie so firmly. He backed off with a grumble, clearly unwilling to re-ignite our argument.

'They're seeing that padre this evening apparently,' he finished, changing the subject innocuously. 'Seemed to have a lot of trouble getting hold of him, though I would have thought that an eighty-five-year-old vicar was pretty easy to track down, even for them.'

I was getting tired of Charlie's supercilious tone, and if truth be told pretty tired of him, in all his obsolescent pomposity.

'Well, let's hope he can tell them something useful,' I said. 'Thanks for the call, Charlie.'

I had been about to tell him of my meeting with David Learmont, and my pet theory about Rowena, but suddenly thought better of it, and of mending fences. The hell with him. It was I think the first time in my life I had ever put the phone down on anyone.

Kate was surprised, but looked at me admiringly. I've always enjoyed it when that happens.

**

The next morning I decided I'd been a bit abrupt with poor old Charlie, and rang him to mend fences. Sam Lane picked up.

'He's not here,' said Sam, when I asked after Charlie. 'His phone diverts to mine when he's out. Got a trustees' meeting in London.'

The Regimental Trustees were not to be taken lightly. To a man (and in 2005 they were all men) they were successful: either in their military careers, like Jazzer, or in other fields once they had left the Army, like me. Not that I was a trustee, but it might come one day. Between them they had a wide span of abilities, which some wore more lightly than others, and were not as a rule shy in demonstrating these. As Colonel of the Regiment Jazzer was not the Chairman (that was generally the previous Colonel), but his appointment made him a key figure. He would undoubtedly be there, probing all the paperwork which the Regimental Secretary had laboriously put together. I knew that Charlie dreaded these meetings, finance not being his strong point.

'He'll be nervous, then,' I laughed.

Sam grunted. 'Almost as much as he was when he had to see the police yesterday. Flapping like a budgie, he was.'

'Yes, he told me about his chat with them,' I replied. 'Not sure why he was so worried about it: he was in Home Headquarters, after all.'

I could hear Sam breathing on the line, but he said nothing. 'Sam?'

'Yes. But I think he was worried about proving it.'

'Well you were there, surely? And Amy? Or Anvi?'

'No. That's the point. I left Home HQ at about 10am to attend a funeral. Went straight home afterwards.'

I knew that Sam was a divorced man, and lived alone.

'Amy, then?' The hairs were beginning to rise on the back of my neck. It's a cliché, but at times like that they really do.

'On leave. She goes to Cyprus every year, always in October: too hot earlier.'

'Anvi?'

'On a finance course in London all that week.'

'So there's only his word for it that he was there all day?'

'After I left – yes. That's what he was worried about.'

'And what did he say afterwards?'

Sam's reply was nonchalant. 'Not worried. He gave me a call last night. I'm pretty sure he thought he'd convinced them he was here. As of course he was.'

'Of course,' I replied. 'Thank you so much, Sam. I'll call Charlie tomorrow.'

I put the phone down, and thought for about ten seconds. Then I returned to the kitchen.

'I heard,' said Kate, before I had a chance to open my mouth. 'I'd say my bet is back in play, wouldn't you?'

***

Kate and I talked things through all morning, and over lunch. Though dubious about Charlie, she was certain the police would pin his location on the day of the murder down without much difficulty, and then if he had questions to answer they would ask them. I wasn't so sure.

'Don't forget, he shoots,' my wife kept saying with annoying regularity.

Despite my own suspicions, I felt a gnawing sense of disloyalty to my old friend. He was of an unusually conventional mindset, even for a former Army officer of his generation – however the thought of him committing a crime as outrageous as murder seemed absurd.

But what if something threatened that highly regimented (and regimental) world he lived in to a fundamental degree? I'm no psychiatrist, but a massive over-reaction in those circumstances didn't seem entirely impossible.

After lunch I walked the dogs for longer than usual whilst turning things over feverishly in my mind. By the time we got home I had come to a decision.

'I'm going to confront him,' I announced. Kate looked at me in disbelief.

'When?'

'This evening. He'll have had a long day in London. He'll go straight home from the station, I'm sure.'

'That's ridiculous,' replied sensible, down-to-earth Kate. 'You aren't some sort of private eye. If you suspect Charlie of anything, then let the police know and they'll investigate. That's their job.'

'I don't want to point the finger at an old friend,' I replied stubbornly. 'There's probably nothing to it. If I drop Charlie in it with the police in those circumstances he'll never forgive me, and rightly so. I need to be sure.'

Kate considered this for a moment.

'What if your suspicions are correct, and Charlie is the murderer? He'll have to shut you up, won't he? And if you're right, he's capable of it. Pretty isolated, that cottage of his, isn't it?'

We'd only been there once, for a rather dubious lunch cooked by our host, but it was true that Charlie's cottage on his former wife's estate was definitely isolated – indeed, although of a different style and surroundings, it was not dissimilar to Georgina's in that respect.

'And don't forget—' began Kate.

'I know. He shoots,' I interrupted.

'Are you going to call him first?' Kate asked.

'No. I'm just going to turn up. If he's there, well and good. If he's not, I'll wait. And if he's not there after a couple of hours he's probably staying in town overnight, so I'll come home, whereupon you'll call me a bloody fool.'

Kate smiled automatically, but I could see she was deep in thought. Suddenly she stood up swiftly from her stool – clearly a decision had been reached.

'Well, we'd better get going,' she announced.

'What do you mean?'

'He's hardly going to kill both of us, is he?' she replied. 'Especially if we make it plain to him from the outset that people know where we are.'

I considered this. My wife had surely experienced more than enough drama for one week – indeed for a lifetime – but she did not seem shaken by it, and indeed what would probably be a tedious chore if I undertook it alone would surely be more akin to an adventure if she accompanied me; something we might laugh about together in our dotage. Plus I was still convinced there was nothing in it: we would probably all settle down for a cheery drink together after any misunderstandings had been cleared up.

'OK. We'll be like the Avengers,' I said.

Kate looked at me quizzically as she headed upstairs to

get ready; I'm not sure she remembered the programme, even though from certain angles she looked very passably like Diana Rigg in her heyday.

I sent a quick email whilst I was waiting. Just insurance, as we'd agreed.

CHAPTER TWENTY-TWO

Charlie lived about ten miles outside Newark – nearer Southwell really – and it was a drive of nearly an hour. Once we'd set off, I suspect we both felt rather foolish: I know I did. Faintly nervous, too.

Neither of us said much until I turned off the A46, and then I sensed Kate brace in her seat.

'Well,' she said. 'Here we go, then.'

I gave her thigh a little squeeze.

'Glad you're here,' I said. And indeed I was. Kate smiled tightly, and gave me her 'you owe me' expression.

It was about four miles to the estate owned by Sian, Charlie's ex, where he still lived in a grace and favour cottage: the unspoken tension in the car ratcheted up a notch as we swept noisily over the cattle grid and through the gates. It was coming up to 5pm on a fine October evening.

Sian's estate was a large one. After about half a mile of rolling parkland, complete with deer (maybe it was a deer grid?) the narrow metalled road to Charlie's cottage led through some woods, laid out for game shooting well over a century before. The pheasant release pens were very prominent as we drove through the woods, and plenty of birds were in evidence so early in the season.

There was a row of four well-maintained semi-detached cottages after the first wood, still occupied by Sian's estate workers, and another 500 yards or so beyond them loomed the second wood, which was more akin to a spinney. I knew from our previous lunch visit that Charlie's rather grander detached cottage, originally built in Edwardian times for the head keeper, lay in a clearing in the middle of this, the road continuing on past it and eventually leading via further woods to another gate on the other side of the estate.

We looked at each other in unspoken trepidation as we entered this second wooded area, travelling of course very slowly because of the pheasants. It was less than a minute before we reached the clearing.

We both saw it at the same time.

'Oh God,' said Kate.

***

Charlie's dark blue Subaru estate was in plain view outside the cottage. I drove up to it and parked alongside, all the while expecting to see him emerge from his front door: it wasn't as if he would have received many unexpected visitors in such an out-of-the-way spot.

'I suppose you felt a bit like this when you visited Georgina?' I asked, as we drew up.

'I was a bit nervous, turning up on spec. But murder was not a consideration,' Kate replied firmly.

'Wonder what we'll find here,' I said, as I opened my car door. Kate was tight lipped as she followed suit.

I knocked on the front door (no bell) whilst Kate hung back a couple of paces. Nothing. This was not a scenario we had envisaged: car present, but no Charlie.

'Well, what now?' Kate said.

After a second's reflection I pulled out my mobile, and called Charlie's. It rang faintly from inside the Subaru. Kate indicated it, and grimaced. I paused again to think.

'Look,' I said, after a moment or two. 'He's been in London all day. He's probably just taking his dog for a walk. It won't have had any exercise, and neither will he. That's what I'd do.'

Kate thought briefly and nodded.

'Let's give him half an hour,' she said.

We got back into my Alfa and sat there quietly as the sun slowly sank towards the horizon, with both front doors open on what was a surprisingly balmy evening for October. Kate turned on the radio, and we listened to the evening news. Being only a few days after the devastating Kashmir earthquake I remember that it wasn't uplifting.

I had parked facing the house, which in retrospect was a mistake. It meant of course that we were oblivious to anyone approaching the car from the rear, unless keeping a close eye on the mirror, and neither could we make a quick getaway. I wasn't, and we couldn't.

So when there was a sudden thump on the roof we both jumped out of our skins.

'Hello, old chum,' said Charlie, in a surprised tone, leaning through my car doorway. 'What the hell are you doing here?'

I was about to reply when I saw what he was carrying.

The shotgun in the crook of Charlie's arm was broken open, as was correct carriage if it was not in use. The chambers of its two barrels gaped empty, though since he had a cartridge bag slung over his shoulder I took little comfort from this: it would be the work of a moment for Charlie to load and close his weapon, whereupon it would be instantly ready to fire as soon as he thumbed the safety catch forward. Beyond this, I knew that the man leaning into my car was unlikely to make a mistake if he decided to put his gun to use.

As all this whirled through my mind there was a pause of at least a second: it still sends shivers down my spine when I recall it. Kate sat frozen by my side. Then I saw that Charlie was smiling broadly. I thought fast.

'Well, Charlie,' I said, mirroring his smile as I extracted myself from the car and stood up. 'I didn't like the way our last telephone call ended. My fault, I think. I came to apologise.'

Charlie looked dumbfounded. His black labrador, Ballad, looked dubiously at me from behind her master's legs.

'What? Nonsense. Just a healthy disagreement; no harm done,' he said. Then he saw Kate.

'My dear,' he said bashfully. 'I am so sorry. I had no idea you were in the car. I must have made you jump.'

Kate nodded her head in acknowledgement, but said nothing. I knew she was scared enough not to trust herself to speak.

'So mutual apologies all round, it seems,' I said, with faux jollity.

'Hah!' replied Charlie cheerily. 'Honours even, then. Come on in!'

He turned towards the door without a backward glance. It didn't appear to be locked, and Charlie vanished inside, Ballad at his heels. I could see Kate mouthing 'No' at me, but it was simply too late to decline. I shook my head and spread my hands in a gesture of helplessness. Then I turned to follow Charlie, Kate's look of horror imprinted on my mind.

You enter Charlie's cottage straight into a hallway, where he'd laid a table when we'd come for lunch a couple of years before. I could see that this was now folded away: it appeared to serve as a sideboard in daily usage, and there were framed pictures of Charlie's two children as toddlers upon it – though very obviously not one of his former wife, Sian. To the right was the drawing room, and the one corner I could see of it from the hall contained an untidy desk, which was clearly Charlie's home office. To the left was the kitchen, and straight ahead just beyond the kitchen door were the stairs, leading up to a small landing where they doubled back to the first floor. It wasn't a complicated layout.

Charlie was in the kitchen, and called me through. His shotgun was propped up in an armchair in the corner, and he was busily laying out newspaper on the unvarnished wooden table. Then he dismantled the gun into its three constituent parts, laid them on the paper and fished in a cupboard for what I recognised as a gun cleaning kit. It went onto the table too, together with a dirty can of WD40 oil.

'Come in; come in,' he called out breezily as he began cleaning the gun. 'Help yourself to a drink. On the side there.'

I sensed Kate appearing cautiously in the doorway behind me as I moved towards the tray on top of the dishwasher.

'Can I get you one, Charlie?' I asked.

'Small whisky. No – the hell with it. Large whisky! Not

driving,' he replied, as he held the barrels up to the light after pulling them through.

'I'll have a very small whisky, because I am driving. Kate?' I said, turning to my wife.

'Something soft, please Dom. Anything.'

I poured her a Diet Coke.

'Just thought I'd take the gun whilst I was walking Ballad after getting back from London,' continued Charlie happily. 'She loves it when I do. Of course, bloody hopeless – no pigeons flighting on an evening like this.'

'Why are you cleaning the gun, then?' asked Kate quietly.

'Over-optimism,' replied Charlie. 'I did shoot at a couple of the buggers in the hope of giving Ballad something to retrieve. Too far. I swear the damn things know the range of a shotgun to the inch. Still, a nice evening to be out and about.'

He finished cleaning the gun, then there was a tremendous ritual around retrieving the keys to the gun cabinet from his safe under the stairs, locking the gun in the cabinet, which was in the boot room leading to the back door off the kitchen, and then returning the gun cabinet keys to the safe. The whole rigmarole took about five minutes.

Meanwhile Kate and I looked on and nursed our drinks whilst Charlie prattled away. Kate visibly relaxed once the gun had gone.

'Come on through,' said Charlie, when all this was complete. 'Let's sit soft. I'm sorry it's a bit untidy. Wasn't expecting company.'

The drawing room contained a sofa, a couple of chairs, Charlie's desk, a small drinks tray and a TV set in the opposite corner. There were chintz curtains which didn't fit very well, still drawn from the night before, and a carpet verging on the threadbare – all no doubt salvage from Charlie's married life.

We sat and contemplated each other in silence: Kate and I on the sofa; Charlie in a chair opposite, with Ballad at his feet. It became rather awkward. To my surprise, it was Charlie who broke the silence.

'Now Dom,' he said, in a kindly tone. 'Please tell me why you are really here.'

***

Kate and I looked at each other. I decided to grasp the bull by the horns. If things turned bad the gun was no longer a factor; I was younger, bigger and stronger than Charlie; and beyond that I had Kate too.

'It's about the murder, Charlie,' I began, and then stopped.

'Ah yes. Terrible business. Especially for you, my dear,' he said, turning to Kate.

'Thank you. It was awful,' replied Kate, in a small voice.

'But what of the wretched murder?' Charlie continued eventually, seemingly bewildered.

I thought carefully before I replied, and phrased it clumsily anyway.

'You were in Home Headquarters on the day, isn't that so, Charlie?' I said.

'Yes – as I told you the other day,' replied Charlie. I fancied he was becoming defensive.

'I assumed that others in Home Headquarters would be able to verify that,' I said. 'The trouble is, nobody can. Isn't that the case?'

Charlie looked astonished as I continued confidently.

'Amy – on leave. Anvi – on a course. Sam – regimental funeral. You were the only one in the office, weren't you?'

'And there's nobody to vouch for you being there all day, is there?' added Kate.

Charlie gasped; horrified: the result of our brilliant detective work I assumed.

'It is not uncommon that there is only one of us there. The other three share an office. It's next door to mine; you've seen it. We cover each other's phones.'

'That's not the point, is it, Charlie?' I persisted.

Charlie went puce in the face. I wasn't sure what was coming next, but was caught unawares by the explosion that did.

'This is tripe of the first order. The police are perfectly aware that I was alone in Home Headquarters – I told them so, as I would have done you if you had cared to ask. Are you seriously suggesting that I, Major Charles Manning, Regimental Secretary of Prince Rupert's Horse, sneaked off that afternoon and shot this poor woman? Why on earth would I?'

Either his indignation was very genuine or he was a damned good actor. I began to feel uncomfortable. Kate looked at me uncertainly.

'As an old friend I did not want to go to the police with any allegation that you were not where you said you were without discussing it with you first: that's the long and short of it,' I said.

Pompously put, as I recognised even at the time. It was definitely my turn to feel defensive.

'Well thank you so much for your consideration, Dom,' said Charlie.

I've never liked sarcasm.

'Because we thought there might be a possibility of you being involved I let someone know we'd be coming here,' I continued. It sounded vaguely sensible, even though my balloon was fast deflating.

'I think you'll find that the police have verified my presence at Home Headquarters through my computer, which I used to send several emails that afternoon,' Charlie responded haughtily. 'I provided them with all the necessary log-in details.'

Kate and I had not considered this possibility. We looked at each other in embarrassment.

'I'm sorry, Charlie,' I began. But I could see that he was already thinking hard about something else.

'Where did you say Sam Lane was?' he asked after a few seconds.

'Funeral, he told me,' I replied. 'I assumed a regimental one.'

Charlie shook his head vigorously.

'There was no regimental funeral that day,' he said. 'Sam told me that he needed the day off to attend to a delicate family matter. I assumed something to do with his ex-wife; he's been having a few issues with her. No mention of a funeral. Of course I granted it.'

The three of us looked at each other, mutual realisation slowly dawning.

'So where was he?' asked Kate, quickest on the draw.

'And further to that – who did you email to say that you were coming here?' said Charlie.

I was struck dumb for at least five seconds before I could answer.

'I told Sam,' I said. 'Bloody hell. I told Sam.'

CHAPTER TWENTY-THREE

Timing; co-incidence; the inevitable result of my naivety – call it what you will. The fact was that only seconds later, whilst we were all still staring aghast at each other, there came the faint sound of a car drawing up on the gravel outside. Charlie moved swiftly to the drawn curtains, pushed them aside slightly and peered through.

'Christ,' he said, leaping back in shock, and letting the curtain drop. 'It's him.'

He paused for a moment and turned swiftly to Kate.

'Get upstairs – now. He has no idea you came with Dom. Get upstairs and keep quiet. We two will handle him.'

Kate looked at me, wide-eyed. I nodded. 'Go on.'

'Go on woman, he'll be here in thirty seconds,' said Charlie urgently.

Kate needed no further bidding. With a brief look at me over her shoulder she scurried away like a startled deer. Luckily the stairs were carpeted, so she vanished up them silently.

We could hear slow, deliberate steps approaching the front door.

'Your gun…?' I began.

'No time,' said Charlie briefly. 'You saw. Gun cabinet. It's like Fort Knox.'

'Play normal,' I urged him.

Charlie's eyes flashed in agreement, and we sat down hastily with our whiskies opposite each other, looking for all the world (we hoped) as if we'd been having a good old yarn. The steps halted in front of the door, and as they did I spotted the giveaway: Kate's glass of Coke was still half full, but I swept it off the table and placed it under the sofa. Charlie blew out his cheeks in relief.

The sharp rap of knuckles. Ballad leapt up and barked.

Charlie was brave, I'll give him that. Still clutching his whisky, and motioning me to stay back, he moved through to the hall, grabbing the labrador by the collar.

'Who is it?' I heard him ask, calmly, as he shut Ballad in the kitchen.

I looked wildly around. There was a small poker by the fireplace – not a very robust one, but if I needed a defensive weapon it was the only thing to hand.

'Charlie, it's Sam,' said the unmistakable voice from the other side of the door. 'May I come in?'

'Of course,' said Charlie, and began opening the door. I could see that he was doing so slowly, so that he could slam it shut if he perceived any sort of threat. But he didn't appear to. I moved into the drawing room entrance behind him as he pulled the door open to its fullest extent.

'Hello Sam,' he said. 'This is rather unexpected.'

Sam stood silhouetted against the darkening evening sky,

wearing an old Barbour jacket: he looked serious, but carried no obvious weapon. He stood stock still, and said nothing until the silence was sufficiently awkward that Charlie was obliged to do so.

'Well, don't just stand there. Come on in. Drink? Dom and I were just having one.'

***

Sam hesitated for a moment, came to a decision and crossed the threshold. He looked at me briefly.

'Hello Dom,' he said. I acknowledged him with a smile, not sure what to say.

'I'll join you in a whisky if I may.'

'Fine,' said Charlie, ushering him through to the drawing room. 'Take a pew.'

Sam ignored him, and stayed standing till he had been handed his whisky, which Charlie poured from the bottle on the tray by his desk.

'Won't you sit down, Sam?' asked Charlie encouragingly.

He indicated the chair he had been sitting in, and I settled into the sofa opposite in the hope that Sam would follow my example.

Instead he paused, seemingly deep in thought.

'No thanks,' he said, with sudden decisiveness. He moved off to lean against the mantelpiece on the other side of the room, took a big pull at his whisky, and then looked hard at us both. It was not an expression I'd seen from Sam before; neither was it one I liked.

'All right,' said Charlie. He perched on the arm of the sofa next to me, completely calm. 'What do you want, Sam?' he asked gently. I could see that he was trying to keep things as low key as possible.

'You've been comparing notes, no doubt?' Sam said accusingly, his eyes flicking between us.

Charlie and I looked at each other.

'Well, we've been putting the world to rights over a dram, Sam, yes,' I said. 'That's what old chums do.'

'Old chums!'

Sam spat the words out bitterly.

'What do you mean, Sam?' Charlie was still doing his sensible 'play it down' act.

'You lot!'

'Please explain, Sam,' I said, adopting Charlie's understated manner.

Though I knew well enough what he meant. Almost all officers in Rupert's came from privileged backgrounds – certainly in 2005. Public school; comfortable upbringing; prosperous white collar parents; university: that was the stereotype. Those commissioned from the ranks like Sam had experienced a harder start in life: though highly respected, inevitably they lacked the social confidence of the upper middle class, with its almost masonic rituals of behaviour. Some made the transition to the officers' mess easily enough, but some didn't, and this could cause resentment.

Generally this was well concealed, but Sam's mask had just slipped. He threw back most of his whisky in one gulp, and looked at me with disdain.

'Reckon Charlie did it, then?' he asked aggressively.

'No,' I replied as calmly as I could. 'He was in Home Headquarters. Though you did tell me he was worried about proving it.'

Sam shrugged, with a grin that was more of a grimace. 'Can't, can he?'

'Actually I can, Sam,' retorted Charlie. 'The police have examined my computer. They are entirely satisfied that I sent several emails from it that afternoon.'

Sam stayed impassive, but there was a bead of sweat on his brow. Maybe it had been there all along, but I hadn't noticed it before.

'So the question, Sam, is where were you?' I said quietly. 'Not at a funeral, which is what you told me.'

'And not what you told me,' added Charlie. 'Then it was some sort of family crisis. I don't think it'll take the police long to recognise that discrepancy.'

Sam stood stock still for a moment. He looked for a second as if he would burst into tears, before moving swiftly over to Charlie's drinks tray and helping himself to another generous measure of whisky – over half the glass. He didn't dilute it.

'Do help yourself,' said Charlie, with a hint of irony, which I thought was unwise. I glanced quickly at Sam. It was lost on him.

He turned to face us.

'I went to see her.'

***

'Tell us what happened, Sam,' I said, as mildly as I could. I could sense my heart beginning to thump in my chest.

'I went to see that journalist woman because she was deliberately going to cause the Montagnon family embarrassment. They didn't deserve it. Fine people. Neither did the Regiment deserve it.'

'Well, you were Jazzer's RSM, I suppose,' mused Charlie.

'I was, and proud to be. And his father was a regimental hero: two DSOs and an MC. He shouldn't have his name tarnished by some muckraking tart.'

He sounded dangerously volatile. Charlie and I glanced at each other, the same sense of bewildered worry.

'Even if there's something in the accusation she was going to make?' I said eventually. 'I think there may well be.'

'Even then,' said Sam tightly.

'How did you know where Georgina lived?' I asked.

Sam waved his free arm and took another pull of whisky.

'A photocopy of the letter she wrote when she replied to your post on the website is in the file. You put it there. It's on headed paper. Easy enough.'

'Did you warn her you were coming?' said Charlie, with every appearance of genuine curiosity.

'No; of course I bloody didn't. Might have been a wasted trip if she hadn't been there. But I knew by the time I arrived that she was. Rang from a phone box when I was a few miles away. Said I'd got the wrong number.'

'Interesting that you did that, and didn't use your mobile,' I said conversationally. 'I'd say that shows a degree of pre-meditation.'

Charlie looked at Sam expectantly, who was draining the dregs of his whisky.

'So you got there, and…?'

'I knocked on the door. She answered. I started explaining why I was there. She tried to slam the door in my face; f-ing and blinding. She was no lady; that one: a real harridan. She was still screeching away in the doorway as I went back to my car. Then she slammed the door shut once I got to it.'

'And in your car you happened to have a shotgun, I suppose?' I asked, as if it was the most natural thing in the world.

Sam looked hunted.

'I'm a wildfowler; it had just been repaired: I'd collected it from the gunsmiths that day… that can be checked.'

It sounded pretty feeble, and Sam looked at us both in turn. He could tell we didn't believe him. Why the ammunition, then? An unspoken question, but he knew what we were thinking.

Sam put his glass down and shrugged; a defeated man.

'I just thought – what a bloody bitch. I thought I might scare her. I'd have had a better plan if I meant to do it.'

Neither Charlie nor I said a word. I don't know what he thought, but I know what I did: *you don't need to load a gun to scare somebody with it.*

'So I went in quietly this time. The door was unlocked. She was in the kitchen. As soon as she saw me she started screaming hysterically. She was heading for the phone. I shot her; one shot. Instinctive. It was enough.'

'Bloody hell, Sam,' said Charlie. 'What now?'

Sam moved back to the mantelpiece; he was over ten feet from us.

He reached into the inside pocket of his Barbour jacket, and my heart leapt as I saw what he pulled out. The German 9mm Luger pistol, a 1908 design, is probably the most recognisable handgun in the world.

'Souvenir?' asked Charlie, as lightly as he could. Sam grinned tightly.

'Won it at cards in Germany – 1985. Still got swastikas on the handgrip.'

1985 was my era. It wasn't particularly unusual for people to have their own handguns then, though obviously they were licensed, and kept in military armouries. Sam's didn't appear to be legally held though, because if it had been he would have had to hand it in for destruction or compensation after the banning of handguns following the Dunblane school massacre in 1996.

'And why have you brought it here?'

It was brave of Charlie to ask – braver than I would have been.

'I had some idea I might need it.' It was hard to judge his mood.

'Now Sam,' said Charlie, standing up. 'Things are bad. You have committed a murder. But they are going to get a damn sight worse if you do anything idiotic with that gun.'

'What are you going to do, commit two more murders?' I asked as I stood up too, eyeing up the distance to the poker.

I could see that Sam was in an agony of indecision.

'He'll have to make it three,' said a tense female voice from the hallway.

***

Sam swung round in shock, his right arm outstretched, pointing the pistol. I was proud of my girl: she didn't flinch.

'You're not going to kill a woman too, are you Sam?' said Charlie scornfully.

'He's done it before, Charlie,' said Kate drily, her eyes fixed on the man threatening her. 'As I know only too well.'

Charlie stared ahead grimly at this reminder of the reality of what Sam had done. The pistol stayed pointed at

Kate for the longest three seconds of my life. Then suddenly Sam lowered it, and turned momentarily away.

Kate made a quick dash to my side from the doorway, though in truth it was only a couple of steps. I felt her hand reach for mine, and though I gave it a quick squeeze I released my hold immediately: if I had to act fast, any encumbrance might be fatal. She looked across at me briefly, seemingly hurt, and I tried to reassure her.

'Brave girl,' I mouthed silently, with as near a smile as I could muster. Her eyes filled with tears.

Sam turned round, clearly at a loss. With a sudden gesture he pulled back on the mechanism of the Luger and then released it: there was a harsh, metallic double click as a bullet was fed into the chamber. The pistol was cocked, and ready to fire. I felt Kate flinch, and saw Charlie brace himself. As for me – I remember thinking even at the time that Sam wouldn't shoot. It struck me more as a gesture to maintain control than a preliminary to killing us.

It was a stand-off: three of us facing a gunman.

'So what now, Sam?' asked Charlie, in a low tone.

Like me, he was leaning forward, body tensed for action. Sam was standing ten feet away. I reckoned there was a fair chance of one of us reaching him without being hit if we made a rush together.

Sam stared grimly ahead, and suddenly raised the pistol again, this time in a two-handed grip, with his arms fully extended in front of him. He pointed it first at Charlie, then at me, then back at Charlie again. He seemed dangerously irrational.

'Don't try anything, you bastards. It won't work,' he said through clenched teeth, as if he could read our minds.

'The police are on their way,' said Kate suddenly. She told me later that she thought it was the moment of maximum danger: she was certain Sam was about to fire.

For a heart-stopping moment the gun swung onto her.

'There's a landline up there, in Charlie's bedroom,' she explained coolly. 'It's got a cordless handset. I heard as much as I needed to, then shut myself in the loo and dialled 999.'

Sam looked indecisive, and for a moment I thought Kate might have overplayed her hand.

'Clever bitch, aren't you?' he sneered.

'Well I'm not a fool, certainly. And I've seen your handiwork. So no option, really.'

I glanced at my wife in admiration. She held Sam's gaze stubbornly.

Suddenly he exhaled: it was more like a deflation really. He moved through the doorway into the hall.

'I'm leaving. Leaving before they get here. Don't follow, or I'll blow your silly heads off.'

And with that he was gone – out into the hall, and seconds later the front door slammed. We looked at each other, stunned, and Kate fell into my arms.

'Well done,' Charlie mumbled to her. He turned to me to explain.

'There isn't a bloody phone upstairs. That took balls – excuse my French.'

He moved back to the curtain, pushing it gently aside.

'He's just wandering around by his car,' he said. 'I think he's trying to decide what to do.'

'Well if nobody turns up soon he'll realise it's a bluff. Then he might come back, angrier than ever. So let's call the police properly this time, and lock ourselves in. I'll call; Kate

– check everything's locked. Charlie – go and get that gun of yours.'

The words were hardly out of my mouth when there was a dull report from outside. Charlie stayed peering through his gap in the curtains for a moment. Then I saw the tenseness in his body visibly drain away.

'No need for any of that,' he said softly, turning back to both of us. 'Except perhaps the police. Look.'

He drew back one of the curtains. Even though it was almost completely dark by then, the body beside the three cars on the pale gravel was all too obvious.

CHAPTER TWENTY-FOUR

After that it was all rather an anti-climax. There was obviously no arrest, and no trial. Inquest procedures loomed, which was tedious, especially for Kate, but it was all a bit of a farce as everyone knew how both Georgina and Sam had died, and who was responsible in each case. Press coverage was surprisingly muted, and the Regiment clearly had no interest in publicising the fact that one of its retired officers had been a suicidal rogue killer.

There were calls between us all of course, and Charlie and I met up with Jazzer in London for a thorough debrief (definitely not in the Cavalry & Guards Club; 'walls have ears' and all that), but beyond that everything began to return to normality quite quickly.

That changed about two weeks later, as I opened my *Telegraph* one morning over breakfast. When I got to the Announcements section I scanned the births, marriages and deaths, as I always do, intending to move swiftly on. Suddenly I was pulled up short.

*STONTON – **Simon Anthony.** Peacefully at home on 5th November, aged 80. Beloved husband of Ann, father of Benedict and Charlotte and proud veteran of Prince Rupert's Horse. A private family funeral has already taken place, and a thanksgiving service to celebrate Simon's life will be held at 3pm on Wednesday 30th November at St Mary Magdalene church, Waltham on the Wolds, Leicestershire LE14 4AH.*

It was then Friday 11 November. I turned to the pile of mail that had arrived with the paper, and as I expected spotted an envelope with the regimental crest. These things are emailed out now, but not in those days: it was indeed notification of Simon's death, sent to all serving and former officers in the Regiment by Home Headquarters, and signed by Charlie Manning. I knew for a fact that Sam Lane had usually drafted them, and felt a momentary pang of amusement at the thought of Charlie unexpectedly having to do so himself.

I hadn't known that Simon had been ill, and maybe he hadn't – there was no indication of cause of death, and there were a couple of cases in my own family of people dying suddenly of heart attacks. But I was genuinely sorry to learn the news.

Kate came into the kitchen after a minute or so, bustling around looking for something.

'Simon Stonton's died,' I said in low-key fashion, indicating the paper to her.

'Who's he?' she replied distractedly, opening a cupboard.

'One of those old wartime regimental chaps I interviewed. You remember – that time I went over to Waltham.'

Kate stopped her foraging and looked at me, having found her errant car keys.

'You went over there a couple of times, didn't you? A nice old boy, you said. I'm sorry.'

She sat down and took my hands in hers.

'Thanksgiving service on the thirtieth. I'd like to go. Will you come?'

'At Waltham? Of course, if you want me to.'

It wasn't always a given that Kate went to funerals, particularly ex-Army ones, so this was a plus, reinforcing how close we'd become since our recent ordeal. When you nearly lose something you value it more, and I think that was much the same for both of us.

Nothing much happened over the next few days – or nothing of import to this story anyway – and 30 November came round quickly enough. We set off after an early lunch to secure a good place in the church; me wearing my regimental tie, as I knew would everyone else who had served in Rupert's. Kate did her normal trick of looking timelessly elegant without much apparent effort. She was hatless, as always. We parked easily enough, and made our way slowly into the church with other prudently early arrivals.

Kate nudged me as we approached the entrance.

'Look,' she said, indicating to the left. 'Two vicars. Wonder why?'

I glanced up idly; the two robed priests were probably thirty yards away by the churchyard wall, engaged in deep conversation. Then I noticed the Military Cross ribbon on the robes of one of them.

Nick Carson.

***

St Mary Magdalene was (and is) not a very large church, and it was filling rapidly. I was glad that we had arrived early, and even more glad that there was a decent turnout for Simon. There were no close friends there, but plenty of former members of Prince Rupert's Horse – a few old men I recognised from reunions, and some who had served with me, but overall I couldn't put a name to more than a dozen or so.

Kate and I found ourselves a good spot in a pew about halfway back on the right-hand side, and settled into the time-honoured ritual of studying the service sheet. All the while of course we kept an eye on the composition of the growing congregation. After a couple of minutes Kate craned around, having picked up on someone's voice. She pulled at my sleeve.

I looked back towards the entrance to see Charlie shake hands with some old boy, exuding bonhomie. It was part of his job to make sure the Regiment was represented at funerals of course, so I wasn't surprised to see him enter the church, particularly as Simon was a former officer who lived reasonably close to Home HQ in Newark.

What I was surprised by was who followed him in.

First came Mary, chic as ever, and looking rather aloof beneath her pill box hat: she took several service sheets from an usher, and turned back gracefully towards the entrance with a wide and rather patronising smile. I could see that she was wearing a regimental brooch.

Jazzer followed her, smiling to all and sundry, and on his arm was an old woman. I recognised her immediately, though it had been nearly twenty years since we had last met: she looked sharp as a tac, peering around with every appearance of keen curiosity. None of her dress sense had gone, that was for sure.

Led by Charlie, who briefly caught my eye, the Montagnon party was guided to a reserved pew on the other side of the aisle, a few rows forward from ours. As they settled in Kate turned to me.

'Is that Rowena?'

I nodded.

'What are they doing here?' she whispered. 'Long way from Wiltshire.'

I was pondering the same thing. Whilst the Colonel of the Regiment did attend quite a few funerals, they tended to be those of senior people, or those who had achieved big things in later life – the great and the good. Simon was a junior wartime officer of no great subsequent distinction.

I shrugged. 'One of his father's former officers, perhaps? Not many left.'

Kate gave me a sceptical look.

'No. *Cherchez la femme*. Rowena insisted.'

Rowena was certainly of Simon's generation. I gave Kate a 'maybe' nod, and she turned back to her service sheet with evident satisfaction at having further exercised her deductive powers.

The church was almost full now. As the choir began an anthem which I didn't recognise the two priests walked down the aisle together and took their places just short of the altar, one either side. Nick Carson looked keenly into the congregation as soon as he had sat down, and acknowledged some acquaintance he had spotted. He smiled. Then he spotted me, reacting courteously but with unmistakable severity. Or maybe it was solemnity. I acknowledged him with a brief nod.

Finally Simon's family took their seats. Ann was on her son's arm, and passed close by me. I didn't catch her eye, but she was smiling at everyone who did. She was followed by the daughter and her husband, and then another woman whom I presumed was the daughter-in-law.

It was a good service, if a conventional one, but then Simon had been a conventional man. Though it was introduced by the incumbent vicar, it was clear that Nick Carson would be the main event, particularly after Simon's son, Benedict, had delivered a very low-key filial oration – though it's not easy to deliver any sort of parental tribute, as I knew only too well.

The sermon – that was Nick's. Simon hadn't implied they had remained close during our discussions, so I wondered why as I watched him make his way to the pulpit after the third hymn.

I didn't have long to wait: indeed, Nick confronted the issue head on.

'Most of you who knew Simon in later life will be wondering who on earth I am,' he began jovially.

There were a few self-conscious laughs, which was no doubt what he intended.

'So I'll tell you,' he continued. 'Simon fought in the war, in a regiment called Prince Rupert's Horse, which I see is well represented here today. He told everyone that although terrible, that brief period in 1944 and 1945 was the high point of his life. His family knew this, and when I was approached to give this sermon today I had no hesitation in accepting. I was the padre of Prince Rupert's Horse at the time, and I can vouch unreservedly for the courage of young officers like Simon. He was nineteen, and I wasn't much more than six years older. His Commanding Officer was a fine man called

Lieutenant Colonel Giles Montagnon. I must mention in passing the presence here of his son, Lieutenant General Sir Jasper Montagnon, now Colonel of Prince Rupert's Horse.'

As I watched Jazzer acknowledge this from his pew with a dignified nod, I felt a bit mystified. My assessment was that there had been a falling out between Giles and Nick; I assumed over the circumstances of Michael Sweetman's death, and hence Nick had resigned his post. Perhaps he was just being gracious after the passage of so many years.

In truth the rest of the sermon was not that inspiring – standard memorial service fare, to the extent that Kate raised a subtle eyebrow at me at one point. I supposed that if Nick didn't know Simon well a degree of blandness was unavoidable. It did the job. At the end, Nick stressed that everyone would be welcome to join the family afterwards at the village hall for refreshments, which made sense: the small Stonton cottage would not have coped.

'Do we have to?' murmured Kate, as we made our way slowly down the aisle after the service, having waited for the family to depart.

'I'm afraid so,' I replied out of the corner of my mouth. She took it well.

***

Waltham village hall is a surprisingly modern and spacious building the other side of the main Melton Mowbray–Grantham road from the church: it's about 300 yards down a side road, with the pub on the corner. I noticed that this was called The Royal Horseshoes – very appropriate for the funeral of an officer in our Regiment. Most people less the immediate Stonton family walked it, since the local vicar had told us that parking there was at a premium.

Those who had left earliest in the front pews were obviously there before us, and that included the Montagnon delegation, with Charlie hovering around them like an attentive moth. They had already exchanged good wishes with the Stonton family, as everyone was queuing up to do, and thereafter looked slightly isolated, with people hesitant to approach them.

We paid our own respects to the widow, flanked by her family: never easy to do with any degree of originality, but Ann gave every appearance of delight at seeing me again as I mouthed my platitudes. She even offered herself for a kiss, somewhat to my surprise.

'What, another one?' murmured Kate out of the corner of her mouth, as we moved off. I gave her a well-deserved pinch on the bottom.

Jazzer caught my eye, and it was only natural that we closed in on him and his party. Mary and Kate gave each other the sort of exaggerated kisses which women who are not overly fond of each other always exchange (why do they do that?), and Jazzer pointedly turned to his mother.

'Mama,' he said rather condescendingly, 'I can't recall if you have met Dominic Mallory: Captain Dominic Mallory, as was. A former regimental officer who lives locally.'

I was prepared for her to have forgotten, but she was sharper than that.

'Of course,' she said mischievously. 'The regimental ball at Detmold in 1987. I think you trod on my foot.'

It was just before I had left the Army: at the time I thought I had got away with it. Clearly not.

'I fear so, ma'am,' I said, taking her hand, and turning to Kate. 'This is my wife, Kate.'

'Oh do stop calling me that, I'm not the Queen: it makes me feel even older than I actually am. How do you do, Kate? I'm Rowena,' she said.

I could sense Kate's amusement at my discomfiture.

'Hello Rowena,' she said coolly, but I knew that tone: she liked the old woman. They began exchanging cheerful pleasantries, and I turned to Mary: Jazzer was talking seriously to Charlie.

'Long way to come.' Not a very original gambit.

Mary shrugged elegantly.

'We knew you'd be here: you and Kate have had a frightful experience. Plus Rowena wanted to.'

One up to Kate's intuition, I thought.

'You know that vicar?' she continued, nodding across the room. 'He married her to her first husband. She pretty much arranged for him to give the sermon today. And he was Giles's padre too, of course.'

'Bit of a mystery around that, isn't there?' I replied.

'What?' she said innocently. I remember thinking that either she didn't know, or she'd make a very good poker player.

'Well – he left. Resigned. And hasn't been back to the Regiment since.'

Mary frowned, and leaned into me.

'I don't know anything about that, Dom,' she whispered. 'And I'm not sure I want to.'

She turned abruptly away: Kate saw the snub, and gave me a quick, questioning glance. I shrugged.

And suddenly there was the man of the cloth himself, homing in on Rowena and kissing her fondly on both cheeks.

They retreated to an alcove in animated discussion, with Mary trailing behind them, looking rather discomfited. I turned to Jazzer, who had appeared beside me. I remember thinking how tired he looked.

'Your good lady seems to have come through all this remarkably well,' he said, nodding at Kate, now chatting happily to Charlie, whom she saw in a new light after our shared experience.

'As do you all, in fact. I am so bloody sorry that Sam's misguided loyalty to me led to... what happened.'

'Yes – she's tough,' I acknowledged. 'No apparent after-effects at all. Brave girl.'

Jazzer was about to reply when we heard Rowena's raised voice.

'That's ridiculous after all this time, and that poor girl's death. He's dead, you tell me? Then you owe them an explanation,' she said, in a tone which brooked no compromise.

Jazzer and I turned, to see Nick Carson facing Rowena with his head bowed. After a pause of a few seconds he seemed to come to a decision, looked around, saw where I was and headed over in determined fashion. I braced myself for I knew not what.

'Dominic,' he said, tugging at my sleeve and pulling me away from the group. 'May I please have a word?'

'Of course,' I replied, mystified, once he had led me into a corner. Not that I had much choice.

'You live near here, don't you?' he said.

'Forty minutes or so south.'

'The right direction for the Montagnons when they head home?'

'Certainly,' I confirmed, still none the wiser. 'They'll be driving pretty much past our door.'

He paused to reflect.

'I owe you an explanation, as Rowena has just said. Everyone really, but you in particular, as you've been probing for weeks, and I've been blanking you. I wonder if you might agree to us all stopping over with you briefly? That is, me, the Montagnons and that Regimental Secretary fellow...'

'Charlie Manning. Well, let me just confirm with my wife, but I'm sure that will be fine,' I said.

Kate had been watching us carefully out of the corner of her eye, and I beckoned her over with a glance. She slid smoothly across, introducing herself to Nick Carson whilst deploying maximum feminine allure.

I explained what Nick had asked. Kate looked at him wide-eyed for a moment, and he returned her stare gravely.

'Of course. That's no problem at all.'

'Thank you so much, Kate,' said Nick Carson, and kissed her hand with old-style gallantry. I don't think anyone had ever done that to my wife before; certainly not me: it quite disarmed her.

Nick moved off towards the Montagnons, and gathered them in. I could see Jazzer and Mary looking across at us uncertainly as he explained, but eventually indicating their assent.

Rowena nodded vigorously, exclaiming 'Excellent', whilst Charlie, standing slightly apart, looked across at me in bewilderment, his mouth beginning to frame a question.

'Don't ask,' I said, staying him with my hand as I moved to his side.

'Just follow us home, and I have a feeling all will be revealed.'

***

It was approaching 5.30 pm when we all managed to extricate ourselves from the village hall, and almost dark: once we had made our way back to the cars, I led off a mixed convoy consisting of the Montagnons' Jaguar, Charlie's Subaru (our last sighting of which Kate and I recalled only too well), and Nick Carson's little French hatchback.

As soon as we were moving, and could speak in privacy, Kate swiftly turned to me.

'What is all this, Dom?' she said. 'Do you know?'

I shook my head. 'No. Just that Nick Carson says that he owes everyone an explanation. Me in particular.'

Kate fell silent for a moment, thinking, and then turned to me thoughtfully.

'Well, it must be something to do with the period you're writing about. When he was padre to the Regiment.'

'I expect so,' I concurred in a neutral tone. In reality my mind was racing, trying to identify possibilities. Kate seemed disappointed, and lapsed into thought again.

'Surely it can't be like Agatha Christie, when all is explained?' she said after a while.

I had rather a suspicion it might be.

'We'll have to wait and see,' I replied tightly.

Kate gave me a look of disgust, and I could sense her brain beginning to whir again. I concentrated on driving, and on not going too fast – I knew from my Army days that if you're at the back of a convoy it's all too easy to get left behind unless the man at the front shows some consideration. I was acutely aware that the oldest man in the slowest car was in that 'tail end' position, and he hadn't been to our home before.

But we were there soon enough; convoy intact. By then it was completely dark. As soon as I had switched off, Kate seized my keys so she could race ahead to prepare a pot of tea, and conceivably some stronger options. Nick Carson was drawing up ten feet away on my side of the car as Kate got out of the passenger seat. She leant briefly back inside.

'Him,' she said, looking pointedly across me at the Peugeot. 'Hercule Poirot. Mark my words.'

Then she was gone, hurrying inside as I greeted our unexpected guests.

CHAPTER TWENTY-FIVE

We set people up with tea, or coffee, or something else (personally I had a decent-sized whisky: I had a feeling I'd need it, and I wasn't driving anywhere): then we all gravitated towards the drawing room without anyone actually suggesting as much. It was a decent size (still is, we haven't moved), and everyone had somewhere to sit.

Once settled we all looked at each other, nonplussed.

I could see Nick Carson reluctantly beginning to lever his aged frame out of the armchair into which he had sunk, but a surprisingly spritely Rowena beat him to it, and took centre stage in front of the fireplace.

'No,' she said firmly. 'I think it's for me to start.'

Nick sank back, seemingly relieved. We were all agog, Rowena's son included, as we waited for her to gather her thoughts. She made a sudden decision, and turned quickly to me.

'You are writing a history of Prince Rupert's Horse in 1944 and 1945, as commissioned by Jasper. Isn't that right, Dominic?'

I shuffled uneasily in my chair. 'Correct.'

'And at some point, you discovered that I had been writing during the war both to Giles and to Michael?'

'Well—'

'Actually it was me that discovered it,' interjected Kate. 'Dom got the letters you wrote to Michael from Georgina, his niece, and the ones you wrote to Jazzer's father from… your son. I compared them. The handwriting was identical.'

She stopped, seemingly worried that she had called Jazzer by his irreverent nickname. Nobody gave a damn, including the man himself.

'What did you deduce from that, pray?' asked Rowena, looking pointedly at Kate.

I rode to the rescue of my flummoxed wife.

'We – I – concluded that you had transferred your affections to another man. A younger man. Whom you subsequently married.'

'I see,' said Rowena drily, playing her cards very close to her chest. I was forced to continue.

'And – well, it seemed that everything followed from that. Georgina found out, made contact with David Learmont, and they convinced each other that Giles had brought about the death of his rival in love. She was going to publish. Sam killed her for it. He thought it was scandalous that Giles could be accused of such a thing: a smear on the Regiment, and one of its heroes.'

I saw that Rowena too was nursing a whisky. She took a sip, and gave a deep sigh.

'Then that poor girl's death was based on a complete misconception,' she said eventually.

We all waited for her to continue. She paused to think.

'First – I did not break things off with Giles when he got back from Africa. He broke them off with me.'

I saw Mary flash a surprised glance at Jazzer beside her on the sofa, who sat impassive. His mother waved her hands impatiently.

'He was thirty-one years old, and had seen more than three years of war. What was I? A girl of barely twenty-one, completely unworldly. Though we'd written to each other all that time, it was plain when we actually met again that he'd outgrown me. He was very nice about it. But he said he thought I'd be happier with someone nearer my own age.'

'So then?' said Jazzer, rather harshly I thought.

'So then, being young and silly, I decided to show him what he was missing. I didn't disappear. There were plenty of young regimental officers about who were keen on female company. Michael Sweetman was charming and handsome. We had fun. I lost my virginity to him. Then I got pregnant,' said Rowena, with a matter of fact shrug.

She looked around the room with a wry smile, taking in the shocked faces and not the least embarrassed.

'It's an old cliché, but a true one. Every generation thinks it invented sex,' she said. 'Rather illogical, when you think about it.'

Mary looked as if she had smelt something particularly unpleasant. Kate and I both saw it; she caught my eye and raised her eyebrows, with the hint of a grin.

'Of course, Michael had no option but to do the decent thing and propose,' continued Rowena. 'That's how it was in those days. And as a fallen woman, my parents made it plain that I had no alternative but to accept, and then to get down the aisle as soon as I could so that the timing of the birth would be approximately decent.'

'Much against my better instincts, I married them on Saturday the 6th of May 1944,' said Nick Carson, rising to his feet. 'Exactly a month before D-Day.'

***

Rowena ceded the floor graciously to her contemporary, who briefly reflected, parsing his hands in front of his chin, before continuing.

'It was all a rush; but everything was then: they weren't normal times. It was obvious that the invasion was imminent; lots of people were getting married for all the wrong reasons. Mainly to sleep together, because most couples did wait then. I tried to dissuade Rowena—'

'You certainly did – and you failed,' said Rowena firmly. 'Of course, Michael and I had already slept together.'

Charlie stared at her, agog. Jazzer was leaning back with his eyes closed, probably wishing he was anywhere else. Mary retained her rotting fish expression. Kate tried to stifle a smile.

Nick Carson was deep in thought. Just as we were all beginning to stir, he came back to life.

'Rowena knows this now, so I'm not telling tales out of school, but I always had reservations about Michael,' he said. 'He seemed to be a good officer, but he had a very high regard for himself, and he was popular with girls. Not always those of the highest reputation. I did not see him as a suitable match for someone like Rowena, even though under sufferance I agreed to conduct the marriage. I thought he would almost certainly be unfaithful, and would cause her a lot of misery. Also I did not believe Michael's heart was in the match. He was trapped by the pregnancy. Both his family and Rowena's expected him to marry her.'

We all looked at Rowena, who gave an indifferent little shrug.

'Nick was right. Beyond the three days leave he was given for our honeymoon, I saw very little of Michael for the remainder of our marriage, but even though nothing was said I was beginning to have creeping doubts.'

'So then we went to war,' said Nick, picking up his narrative. He paused again.

'It was brutal, even for those who had been in the desert, because we were mostly in close country, which they weren't used to. We started taking serious casualties very early on, including the Commanding Officer. Giles took over. Undoubtedly the right man.'

Jazzer was paying close attention now that we had moved on from his mother's matrimony: military matters had come to the fore.

'Michael – well, Michael was an effective Troop Leader, which not all of those young boys were,' continued Nick. 'But rumours started circulating early.'

'What sort of rumours?' interjected Jazzer abruptly.

I sensed that Nick was struggling with himself. He came to a decision.

'Michael was in A Squadron, under Tommy Cowlam. The Wolf knew enough to keep him out of C Squadron with Giles. Tommy was quite a diffident man, but nonetheless well respected. One evening, three weeks or so after Giles had taken over the Regiment, Tommy asked to see him when we were in leaguer after a very long day.'

We all waited silently for him to continue, sensing that

this was a critical part of the story.

'Tommy told Giles that Michael's Troop Sergeant had reported unacceptable behaviour,' Nick said eventually: it gushed out with something like relief. He seemed to be waiting for a reaction.

'How do you know?' I asked. 'And what constituted unacceptable behaviour?'

Jazzer nodded at me briefly; supportive of the questions.

Nick spread his hands expressively.

'I had many conversations with Giles once he had taken over. Lonely job, and there I was in Regimental Headquarters. He began to use me as a sounding board. That was the first time.'

'What was the issue?' asked Jazzer, as matter-of-fact as ever.

'Women, initially,' replied Nick. 'A couple of local girls in a village where his Troop was billeting overnight when the Regiment was temporarily out of the line were rewarding their liberators in the oldest way, if you know what I mean. Young soldiers don't look gift horses like that in the mouth. Rather than back up his Sergeant when he tried to put a stop to this, Michael encouraged it. Possibly even took part himself; Tommy wasn't sure. He thought the Colonel should know, and wanted his advice. Unbecoming behaviour for an officer.'

'So what happened?' said Mary, seemingly aloof from such tawdriness, although in retrospect I think that was just her natural look.

'Giles spoke to Michael at the next opportunity. Not formally: what the Army then called an "interview without coffee".'

'Still does!' said Charlie, with a grin, and looked around. Nick ignored him, as did everyone else.

'The importance of discipline; setting an example – that sort of thing. Of course he felt protective of Rowena too, as he later told me.'

'And that was that, was it?' said Jazzer, with a hint of cynicism.

'Yes – until the next thing,' replied Nick.

We all waited for him to continue. Nick drew a breath, and continued his explanation of events sixty-one years ago.

'Tommy exchanged Michael's Troop Sergeant for someone else in A Squadron, because that relationship had broken down. That was fine for a couple of weeks, and then the Regiment went off to support the Canadians. They were facing the 12th SS Panzer Division. Does anyone know about them?'

This was clearly a Jazzer moment; we all turned to him automatically.

'Made up mainly of fanatical Hitler Youth boys. Seventeen – maybe eighteen years old.'

Nick continued his narrative.

'They had massacred a lot of Canadian prisoners very early on. Although it was being stamped on, very few SS prisoners were then being taken by the Canadians as a result – fairly common knowledge now, but not then. Our people were rather shocked by what they encountered. However, Michael allegedly adopted that mindset all too easily.'

'Says who?' asked Jazzer. Nick turned to him, it seemed to me with some condescension.

'His new Troop Sergeant raised concerns, first with the Squadron Sergeant Major, and then with Tommy himself. Nothing was ever absolutely substantiated, but the suspicion was definitely there. Michael's tank crew wouldn't talk: they were loyal to him.'

'What did Giles do?' inquired the woman who had been married to both protagonists in this saga.

'I discussed the situation with him, and he settled on what I thought was a rather good solution for everyone. The Regiment had a Recce Troop, which worked directly for Regimental Headquarters. Tough job, probing for information. Johnny Vaughan had done it very well since the beginning, and had recently been posted off to be ADC to some General – not least because I had suggested to Giles that he needed a rest. I sometimes did that.'

'You did it with Simon Stonton,' I interjected.

Nick paused, and nodded at me gravely. 'I did indeed. Later on. Anyway,' he said, 'to continue. Giles decided to post Michael to Recce Troop. That would get him out of A Squadron, where he had clearly burnt his boats, and under Giles's personal supervision. And it was a very credible appointment: Michael was known to be effective.'

The suspense in the room was tangible.

'It worked well, and Michael did a fine job for a long time. Until...'

He stopped. 'Would you mind if I had a little think about this for five minutes?'

***

Kate and I bustled around as good hosts, topping up drinks and cups of tea, and all the while I kept a close eye on Nick, seated stock still with his eyes closed on the bum warmer near the fireplace.

I thought he might even be praying. After about five minutes everyone settled down again, and fell silent. With a small start, Nick realised that we were all waiting for him. He stood up again.

'Michael Sweetman died on the 24th of March 1945,' he began. 'And now I am going to tell you how that came about.'

None of us moved; you could have heard the proverbial pin drop.

'We were crossing the Rhine, North of Wesel – Operation Plunder, one of Monty's great set pieces. Huge artillery support; massive air cover during daylight. The river was about four hundred yards wide. Fantastic effort by the Engineers to bridge it. The infantry, who were Scottish as I recall, had got across earlier in amphibious Buffalo personnel carriers and secured a toehold.'

'When the first of our people got across, the bridgehead was not yet secure: it was only a mile or so deep. Recce Troop led. The others were being moved across the bridge by a Regulating HQ, run I believe by the Military Police. It was like a well-organised traffic jam. Everyone had to wait their turn to be called forward. I asked Giles if I could cross; he agreed, and Trooper Ryan and I blistered on to some medics who were needed the other side in our jeep. It was just getting dark. The Germans were putting in a counter attack, trying to drive us into the river. They were mostly paras – tough boys; we'd met them before.'

He paused again to take stock.

'It was pretty chaotic when we got over the other side, but within a couple of hundred yards I came across a Stuart light tank by the side of the road. It didn't seem to be damaged – just broken down I think. Stuarts were only used by Recce

Troop, so I knew it was them. The Corporal commanding it said that the rest of the Troop were probing forward towards a village. There had been a lot of firing from up there, and I later learnt that Michael and one other tank had bumped head on into the attacking German infantry. They stopped them dead with machine gun fire. They had also captured three men, one of them an officer.'

I could see that he was struggling with how to phrase what followed.

'There was sporadic firing going on still, and we probably went further forward than we should have done, but I knew that Michael would always have at least one tank on the road. We stopped when we saw another Stuart. I have no idea where our infantry were; in woods like that by rights Michael's tanks should have had their protection. Everything seemed quiet, and after a while we closed up to it. I could see from the callsign board on the back of the turret that it was Michael's own tank. It appeared to be deserted, and I told Ryan to stop behind it, rather at a loss what to do. We were quite a few yards back, because tanks have a nasty habit of reversing without warning.

'Then there was some small-arms fire close by, from the woods to our left. Ryan and I got out of our jeep and took cover behind the engine block on the other side. Two people emerged from the wood, and they were laughing. One of them was Michael, and he was carrying a sten gun. The other man was a Lance Corporal, and he was just holstering a revolver. Michael stopped uncertainly in the half-light when he saw us, then waved his companion away, who began climbing back into the tank.

'I remember that Michael said "good evening", but

knowing full well he that he didn't mean it. He didn't like us being there. I asked him what he had been firing at, though I knew already. I have thought about that moment many times since, and his manner was what I would call defiant guilt. "What do you bloody think?" he sneered. I instantly sensed Tom Ryan's shock that anyone would speak to me like that.

"'You have been shooting prisoners," I said. It was not a question. "Necessity," he replied coolly. "We could be attacked again at any moment. What would you have me do with them?" He indicated the small, four-man Stuart tank. "Hardly room in there." I paused, stumped for an instant reply, and he laughed unpleasantly. "Of course, you have the luxury of not having to make such moral judgments, padre, don't you?" he said.

"'Whatever I did, I wouldn't laugh about killing in cold blood," I replied. It was the best I could do. The arrogant smile faded in an instant. "Oh fuck off, Nick," said Michael. His last words.'

'Because then the German artillery crashed in, precursor to a probable resumption of their attack. Ryan and I dived into the ditch on one side of the road, and Michael the other; the tank was between us and just ahead, closed down. Artillery fire is a terrible thing to experience: every shell seems to be aimed at you personally. I huddled there helplessly, waiting for the inevitable. And then I became conscious of Tom Ryan by my side, levering himself out of the ditch and ducking down as he sprinted towards the other side of the road. He had something in each hand.

'The shelling stopped as soon as it had started, which was often the way, though my ears still rang from the explosions.

247

After a moment I crawled out of the ditch and crouched hesitantly in the lee of the jeep, which had a smashed windscreen. The air reeked with cordite. Ryan was five yards away, staring into the opposite ditch. I had never seen an expression of such pure venom on anyone's face.

'As soon as I reached the side of the ditch and looked down I could see that Michael was dead. Ryan turned to me grimly, and showed me his single remaining grenade. I had no idea he even carried any.

'I had a decision to make, and I made it. We had seconds only to act before Michael's crew started looking for him.

'"Quick, pull him out of the ditch and put him on the road," I ordered. Ryan looked at me in astonishment, but did so. Then we both leant over the body.

'"Too late," I said sorrowfully, rising to my feet as Michael's gunner emerged from the turret. I recognised him as the man I had seen earlier. "That last shell got him."

'No doubt a post mortem would have shown fairly conclusively that Michael had died from grenade fragments rather than shell splinters, but people weren't surprised by sudden death in 1945. They encountered it daily, and didn't concern themselves over much with the form it came in for others. The Lance Corporal nodded grimly and sank down into his turret, no doubt to report the loss of his Troop Leader on the radio.

'Ryan and I looked at each other, silent conspirators. We were the only two people who appreciated what had happened. I knew that there had to be a third.'

***

'So Sweetman was murdered, after all,' stated Jazzer flatly. 'Just not in the way everyone seems to have suspected.'

'Yes,' said Nick, simply.

I glanced at Rowena. She exhibited no sign of shock, unlike everyone else: she already knew.

'And the third person in on it was…?' began Charlie.

'Giles, of course,' replied Nick. 'I told him as soon as I had the chance, which wasn't for nearly twenty-four hours.'

Nobody said anything. We all waited for him to continue.

'We'd taken the village outside which Michael had been killed by then. Regimental Headquarters was established in the old schoolhouse – or what was left of it. Giles was in conference with the Adjutant, Alastair Gill, when I arrived, and normally I would not have intruded on that, but he clearly saw something in my expression which caused him to pause. "Yes Nick, what is it?" he asked.

"Can I please see you as soon as possible, Colonel?" I asked him. "Alone."

'I saw Alastair glance at the Commanding Officer, in case he wanted rid of this pestilent priest. Giles stayed him with his hand. "Of course. Nothing like the present. Follow me," he said, and led me into what had once probably been a small storeroom. Now it had been kitted out as Giles's bedroom. As soon as I had closed the door behind me and turned around, I found Giles very close. He did not look pleased.

'"Well?" he said. "Be quick. I have a war to run." I took a deep breath. "Michael Sweetman was killing prisoners again, not far from here. I confronted him. He did not take it well, and words were exchanged. Just then we were hit by an enemy barrage. Ryan killed him with a grenade whilst he took cover in a ditch."

Giles could be pretty inscrutable, but I fancied I saw a slight flicker of astonishment cross his face. He paused for a moment.

"'I heard he was dead. Does anybody else know this?" he asked.

"No," I replied. "Michael's tank was close by, but it was ahead of us, and closed down. Nobody saw. We told the crew he had been caught in the barrage. They accepted it without question."

Giles turned away, and I could sense he was deep in thought, but only for ten seconds or so. Then he moved swiftly towards the door.

"Adjutant," he called. Alastair appeared as if by magic. "Padre Carson has resigned from his post with the Regiment," Giles stated. "Effective forthwith. Arrange for his immediate posting and replacement."

'The door slammed shut on the startled Alastair, and Giles turned quickly to me. "Best I can do," he said. "You don't have to give a reason; just stick to that line. And take bloody Trooper Ryan with you."'

We all sat there, slack jawed. Nick spread his hands, almost apologetically.

'So that's what happened. I've never kept in touch, or been back to the Regiment, because I didn't want to have to explain the inexplicable. And I was concerned for Tom Ryan, of course. But he's been dead three years now.'

CHAPTER TWENTY-SIX

There was a rather uneasy silence as we all digested this. Jazzer broke it.

'Did you know, Mama?' he said, turning suddenly to his mother.

I saw Rowena brace herself.

'No. I had no idea until Nick told me. I thought Michael was just another victim of the war. Tragic that it happened so late on, of course, but it was the same for a lot of people. My parents had the baby adopted straightaway. I didn't have much say in it, and in truth once I'd digested the situation I wasn't sorry. Life could start again. I was still only twenty-three.'

'So when did you—' began Kate.

'What?' retorted Rowena, her hard stare a challenge.

'Well – get together with Giles I suppose,' said Kate sheepishly. From the moment she'd discovered it I knew she had been fascinated by the dynamics of that apparent eternal triangle.

Rowena considered the question seriously.

'After the war Giles left the Army, and turned to farming. But he was always very considerate of "his" widows – those of the officers and men who had died under his command. And I'd grown up a lot too. I suppose we were gradually drawn together. It wasn't a grand passion, but I admired and liked him. One day he proposed. I couldn't see any good reason to say no. I was twenty-eight by then: getting on. And in the main we were very happy.'

'Glad to hear it,' said Jazzer heavily. His mother looked at her only acknowledged son as if he was seventeen.

'And so – David?' asked Mary quietly. It was Nick who answered.

'David's researches led him to me, because I'd married his parents. He wanted to find his birth mother. When he first wrote to me I didn't even know he existed, let alone that he had been given up for adoption. Though I had not seen Rowena since the day she married Michael I wrote to her to tell her of this rather strange approach. Of course I knew that she had subsequently married Giles.'

'Weren't you invited to the second wedding?' asked Jazzer.

I glanced quickly at Rowena, who seemed completely unperturbed. Nick answered calmly.

'Giles asked me, which was very good of him. But I decided it was best that I stayed away from anything to do with the Regiment, as I had done since the war. I was still very wary of the truth coming out, and protective of Tom, who was of course still alive then.'

'You wrote a very charming letter though,' said Rowena. Nick smiled briefly in acknowledgement.

'This Learmont man,' began Jazzer, looking at his mother.

'My half-brother I suppose. Did he contact you?'

'He wrote earlier this year, but I ignored it. I didn't want to resurrect all that, or have to explain it.'

Mary looked at her mother-in-law with what looked very much like shock.

'And there it would have rested, I suppose,' I said, 'until Georgina got in touch with David.'

'I put them in touch,' said Nick simply. 'She somehow found me, wanting to know more about her uncle. She didn't say anything about being a journalist. They were cousins. I thought it was the right thing to do. I'll regret it till the day I die.'

'You weren't to know,' I replied. 'She told David about the matching letters, and together they became convinced that Michael's death had been set up by Giles.'

'Good story for her, of course,' mused Jazzer.

I saw Kate blushing slightly at her role in bringing this about, of which only I was aware. Jazzer turned meaningfully to his mother.

'I am going to meet this half-brother of mine.'

Rowena shrugged briefly. 'As you wish, Jasper. At this stage, I have no desire to. But you may tell me what you think once you have done so.'

This seemed quite a concession from the tough old lady, who actually looked rather emotional. Mary looked supportive of her husband; Kate and I (plus probably Nick too) simply felt embarrassed until Charlie rescued us, oblivious to Montagnon family dynamics.

'I think in his heart-of-hearts Sam believed in Colonel Giles's guilt,' he said. 'He thought he'd prevent a regimental scandal by talking Georgina out of publication.'

'It was a warped loyalty to me, and to my family,' said

Jazzer, shaking his head. Normally so vibrant, for once he looked his age. 'You are too generous, Charlie. I agree he was trying to protect us, but nobody takes a shotgun along if they only intend to persuade.'

Charlie accepted the rebuke humbly. His stature had grown in recent days, I thought: certainly with me. He'd behaved bravely when confronted by Sam, but couldn't quite abandon his personal fondness for his late assistant.

I respected that.

***

'May I ask a question?' It was Mary, and she was looking pointedly at Rowena.

'Of course,' replied Rowena coolly.

'Why wouldn't you say where you'd gone on the day of the murder?'

Rowena looked impatient. 'Surely it is obvious where I went?'

Nick stepped in. 'I had told Rowena about David's approach to me. She wanted to confer once she had been approached by him herself, which happened some weeks later. I agreed to meet her. I told her about Georgina, because Dominic had mentioned her to me, and the suspicion which I thought was forming in her mind after she and David met, because David had told me about that. And also the possible publicity. Of course we happened to meet on the actual day of the murder.'

'Nick told me what actually happened to Michael; as you've just heard,' said Rowena. 'So I knew Giles had nothing to do with it. He didn't want his own involvement known in any way. I felt honour bound by that, because of the Ryan aspect.'

'Though I didn't tell you he was dead, did I?' continued Nick.

'No,' said Rowena pointedly. 'I only learnt that this afternoon. That is why I pushed for this meeting.'

Suddenly there was silence.

'There was no need to protect Tom anymore,' said Nick humbly. 'I just tried to keep the whole thing hushed up out of habit I'm afraid. It has hung over me for sixty years. I am fallible. I apologise.'

'Understandable,' said Jazzer quietly. 'And thank you for being such a fine support to my father.'

***

After that everyone was rather at a loss: Kate said she would rustle up scrambled eggs, but Jazzer forestalled that, decisive as ever.

'Thank you; no: we have already imposed ourselves enough. We must be off.'

After the normal 'are you sure?' ritual Kate led the Montagnons to the front door. She kissed Mary goodbye – a rather friendlier exchange than their earlier one I fancied – and then turned hesitantly to Rowena, whom she had met for the first time only a few hours before. She began proffering her hand. The old lady was having none of it: she pulled Kate into a tight hug.

'Thank you so much, my dear. You have been very kind. I hope you don't think I am too awful?'

Kate smiled and shook her head. As the two female Montagnons made their way to the car, Jazzer took my wife gently by the elbow in the doorway and turned her to face him.

'Dom and Charlie have told me how bravely you conducted yourself that evening, Kate,' he said. 'Nobody could have done better. Well done indeed; we are all proud of you.'

Charlie appeared cheerfully behind him.

'We could say she was a regimental veteran, couldn't we Colonel?' he asked.

Jazzer grinned, in his best old style. 'I entirely concur. And a proven one.'

Kate looked shyly at the ground – most unlike her. But I could see her blush of pleasure.

I signalled my approval to both of them with a brief nod before Kate looked up again.

'Thank you both so much,' said Jazzer simply, making eye contact with each of us in turn. He turned briefly to Nick Carson and shook his hand.

'I'll be in touch.'

As he walked to the car, he summoned me alongside him.

'How's the writing going, Dom?' he asked quietly.

'Barely begun, in truth,' I replied. 'You said I had three years. It's only been a few months.'

We had reached the car.

'That's fine. I don't suppose you need make too much of the Sweetman episode?' he asked, turning to look directly at me as he opened the driver's door.

'No,' I responded. 'But what I do write will be accurate.'

Jazzer accepted this with a brief nod, then paused and looked back at Charlie.

'We'll speak,' he called out, and within a few seconds the Jaguar's tail lights were receding down the drive.

***

Nick Carson was saying his farewells to us when Charlie detached himself and headed for his Subaru: I remember thinking at the time that it would be rather rum if he was heading off without another word. But he was back in seconds.

'This is yours, I believe,' he said solemnly, handing a small black book over to the old priest.

Surprise, shock, and deep emotion registered successively on the recipient's face as he examined what he had been presented with.

Nick looked up at all three of us, lower lip trembling. He turned to his car without another word, raising his hand in a gesture of farewell.

Kate knew nothing of the prayer book which Nick had left behind in 1945, so we had to explain that to her once he had left.

'I knew he was doing the address, and depending on how things went I thought there might be an opportunity to return it to him,' explained Charlie. 'So I put it in the car and decided to play it by ear.'

He looked at us bashfully, as if we might disapprove.

Kate turned to look directly at him, hands on hips.

'You know, Charlie Manning,' she declared forcefully, 'you are actually not a bad chap.'

Charlie smiled briefly, and then a thoughtful looked crossed his face. I thought we might be about to hear something profound.

'I don't suppose those scrambled eggs are still on offer?' he asked.

EPILOGUE

Over a year later I was running yet again through the edited manuscript of my 1944–45 history of Prince Rupert's Horse as a precursor to the typesetting process. I hadn't needed three years.

Theoretically authors shouldn't make changes at this late stage of producing a book, but one phrase jumped out at me.

'On the 24th of March Lieutenant Michael Sweetman, Recce Troop Leader, was killed by enemy artillery fire whilst defending the bridgehead over the River Rhine near the village of Bochander.'

It took me only a few seconds to make the change.

'On the 24th of March Lieutenant Michael Sweetman, Recce Troop Leader, died during an enemy artillery barrage whilst defending the bridgehead over the River Rhine near the village of Bochander.'

I sent the change off to the long-suffering and no doubt mystified publisher, with an apology.

It was a regimental history, and hopefully a definitive one.

And as I had promised Jazzer, it would be accurate. Or what would be the point?

***

A few weeks after that, once my regimental history had gone to the printers, my darling Kate asked me one evening if I had any further writing ambitions.

'I think I might write about last year – what happened,' I replied. 'If you don't mind.'

She smiled, nodded, and reached out across the kitchen island to take my hands.

'Of course.'

So I have done. And this is it.